The huge bulk of the alien capital ship was i̶ ̶ ̶rner of the screen. Level 10, here we come . ̶ ̶ ̶ful . . . there were no more ships now. ̶ ̶ ̶o was keep out of its range and th̶ ̶ ̶ ̶ ̶ish to talk.

Johnny blinked at ̶ ̶ ̶ ̶een.

We wish to talk.

The ship roared by ̶ ̶yooowwwnn. He reached out for the throttle key and slowed himself down, and then turned and got the big red shape in his sights again.

We wish to talk.

His finger hovered on the Fire button. Then, without really looking, he moved it over the keyboard and pressed Pause.

Then he read the manual.

Only You Can Save Mankind, it said on the cover. 'Full Sound and Graphics. The Ultimate Game.'

A ScreeWee heavy cruiser, it said on page 17, could be taken out with seventy-six laser shots. Once you'd cleared the fighter escort and found a handy spot where the ScreeWee's guns couldn't get you, it was just a matter of time.

There was nothing in the manual about messages . . .

ONLY YOU CAN SAVE MANKIND

TERRY PRATCHETT

CORGI BOOKS

ONLY YOU CAN SAVE MANKIND
A CORGI BOOK 0 552 13926 2

First published in Great Britain by Doubleday,
a division of Transworld Publishers Ltd.

PRINTING HISTORY
Doubleday edition published 1992
Corgi edition published 1993
Corgi edition reprinted 1993 (twice)

Set in Monotype Bembo by
Phoenix Typesetting, Ilkley, West Yorkshire

Corgi Books are published by Transworld Publishers Ltd.,
61–63 Uxbridge Road, Ealing, London W5 5SA,
in Australia by Transworld Publishers (Australia) Pty. Ltd.,
15–25 Helles Avenue, Moorebank, NSW 2170,
and in New Zealand by Transworld Publishers (N.Z.) Ltd.,
3 William Pickering Drive, Albany, Auckland.

Printed and bound in Great Britain by
Cox & Wyman Ltd., Reading, Berks.

*Yet another one
for Rhianna*

The Mighty ScreeWee™ Empire™ is poised to attack Earth!

Our battleships have been destroyed in a sneak raid!

Nothing can stand between Earth and the terrible vengeance of the ScreeWee™!

But there is one starship left... and out of the mists of time comes one warrior, one fighter who is the last Hope of Civilization!

YOU!

YOU are the Savior of Civilization. You are all that stands between your world and Certain Oblivion. You are the Last Hope.

Only You Can Save Mankind!™

Action-Packed with New Features! Just like the Real Thing! Full-Color Sound and Slam-Vector™ Graphics!

Suitable for IBM PC, Atari, Amiga, Pineapple, Amstrad, Nintendo. Actual games shots taken from a version you haven't bought.

1

The Hero With A Thousand Extra Lives

Johnny bit his lip, and concentrated.

Right. Come in quick, let a missile target itself – *beep beep beep beebeebeebeeb* – on the first fighter, fire the missile – *thwump* – empty the guns at the fighter – *fplat fplat fplat fplat* – hit fighter No. 2 and take out its shields with the laser – *bwizzle* – while the missile – *pwwosh* – takes out fighter No. 1, dive, switch guns, rake fighter No. 3 as it turns *fplat fplat fplat* – pick up fighter No. 2 in the sights again up the upcurve, let go a missile – *thwump* – and rake it with—

Fwit fwit fwit.

Fighter No. 4! It always came in last, but if you went after it first the others would have time to turn and you'd end up in the sights of three of them.

He'd died six times already. And it was only five o'clock.

His hands flew over the keyboard. Stars roared past as he accelerated out of the mêlée. It'd leave him short of fuel, but by the time they caught up the shields would be back and he'd be ready, and two of them would already have taken damage, and . . . here they come . . . missiles away, wow, lucky hit on the first one, die die die!, red fireball – *swsssh* – take shield loss while concentrating fire on the next one – *swsssh* – and

9

now the last one was running, but he could outrun it, hit the accelerator – ggrrRRRSSHHH – and just keep it in his sights while he poured shot after shot into – *swssh*.

Ah!

The huge bulk of their capital ship was in the corner of the screen. Level 10, here we come . . . careful, careful . . . there were no more ships now, so all he had to do was keep out of its range and then sweep in and *We wish to talk.*

Johnny blinked at the message on the screen.

We wish to talk.

The ship roared by – *eeeyooowwwnn*. He reached out for the throttle key and slowed himself down, and then turned and got the big red shape in his sights again.

We wish to talk.

His finger hovered on the Fire button. Then, without really looking, he moved it over to the keyboard and pressed Pause.

Then he read the manual.

Only You Can Save Mankind, it said on the cover. 'Full Sound and Graphics. The Ultimate Game.'

A ScreeWee heavy cruiser, it said on page 17, could be taken out with seventy-six laser shots. Once you'd cleared the fighter escort and found a handy spot where the ScreeWee's guns couldn't get you, it was just a matter of time.

We wish to talk.

Even with the Pause on, the message still flashed on the screen.

There was nothing in the manual about messages. Johnny riffled through the pages. It must be one of the New Features the game was Packed With.

He put down the book, put his hands on the

keys and cautiously tapped out: Die, alein scum/

No! We do not wish to die! We wish to talk!

It wasn't supposed to be like this, was it?

Wobbler Johnson, who'd given him the disc and photocopied the manual on his dad's copier, had said that once you'd completed level 10 you got given an extra 10,000 points and the Scroll of Valour and moved on to the Arcturus Sector, where there were different ships and more of them.

Johnny *wanted* the Scroll of Valour.

Johnny fired the laser one more time. *Swsssh.* He didn't really know why. It was just because you had the joystick and there was the Fire button and that was what it was *for*.

After all, there wasn't a Don't Fire button.

We Surrender! PLEASE!

He reached over and, very carefully, pressed the Save Game button. The computer whirred and clicked, and then was silent.

He didn't play again the whole evening. He did his homework.

It was Geography. You had to colour in Great Britain and put a dot on the map of the world where you thought it was.

The ScreeWee captain thumped her desk with one of her forelegs.

'*What?*'

The First Officer swallowed, and tried to keep her tail held at a respectful angle.

'He just vanished again, ma'am,' she said.

'But did he accept?'

'No, ma'am.'

The Captain drummed the fingers of three hands on

the table. She looked slightly like a newt but mainly like an alligator.

'But we didn't fire on him!'

'No, ma'am.'

'And you sent my message?'

'Yes, ma'am.'

'And every time we've killed him, he comes back . . .'

He caught up with Wobbler in Break.

Wobbler was the kind of boy who's always picked last when you had to pick teams, although that was all right at the moment as the PE teacher didn't believe in teams because they encouraged competition.

He wobbled. It was glandular, he said. He wobbled especially when he ran. Bits of Wobbler headed in various directions; it was only on *average* that he was running in any particular direction.

But he was good at games. They just weren't the ones that people thought you ought to be good at. If ever there was an Inter-Schools First-One-To-Break-The-Unbreakable-Copy-Protection-on-*Galactic-Thrusters*, Wobbler wouldn't just be in the team, he'd be *picking* the team.

'Yo, Wobbler,' said Johnny.

'It's not cool to say Yo any more,' said Wobbler.

'Is it rad to say cool?' said Johnny.

'Cool's always cool. And no-one says rad any more, either.'

Wobbler looked around conspiratorially and then fished a package from his bag.

'*This* is cool. Have a go at this.'

'What is it?' said Johnny.

'I cracked *Fighter Star TeraBomber*,' said Wobbler. 'Only don't tell anyone, right? Just type FSB. It's not much good, really. The space bar drops the bombs, and . . . well . . . just press the keys, you'll see what they do . . .'

'Listen . . . you know *Only You Can Save Mankind*?'

'Still playing that, are you?'

'You didn't, you know, *do* anything to it, did you? Um? Before you gave me a copy?'

'No. It wasn't even protected. Didn't have to do anything except copy the manual. Why?'

'You did play it, didn't you?'

'A bit.' Wobbler only played games once. Wobbler could watch a game for a couple of minutes, and then pick up the joystick and get top score. And then never play it again.

'Nothing . . . funny . . . happened?'

'Like what?' said Wobbler.

'Like . . .' Johnny hesitated. He could tell Wobbler, and then Wobbler would laugh, or not believe him, or say it was just some bug or something, some kind of trick. Or a virus. Wobbler had discs full of computer viruses. He didn't do anything with them. He just collected them, like stamps or something.

He could tell Wobbler, and then somehow it wouldn't be real.

'Oh, you know . . . funny.'

'Like what?'

'Weird. Um. Lifelike, I suppose.'

'It's *sposed* to be. Just like the real thing, it says. I hope you've read the manual properly. My dad spent a whole coffee break copying that.'

Johnny gave a sickly grin.

'Yes. Right. Better read it, then. Thanks for *Star Fighter Pilot*—'

'*TeraBomber*. My dad brought me back *Alabama*

Smith and the Jewels of Fate from the States. You can have a copy if you give me the disc back.'

'Right,' said Johnny.

'It's OK.'

'Right,' said Johnny.

He never had the heart to tell Wobbler that he didn't play half the games Wobbler passed on. You couldn't. Not if you wanted time to sleep and eat meals. But that was all right because Wobbler never asked. As far as Wobbler was concerned, computer games weren't there for playing. They were for breaking into, rewriting so that you got extra lives or whatever, and then copying and giving away to everyone.

Basically, there were two sides to the world. There was the entire computer games software industry engaged in a tremendous effort to stamp out piracy, and there was Wobbler. Currently, Wobbler was in front.

'Did you do my History?' said Wobbler.

'Here,' said Johnny. ' "What it was like to be a peasant during the English Civil War." Three pages.'

'Thanks,' said Wobbler. 'That was quick.'

'Oh, in Geog last term we had to do one about What it's like being a peasant in Bolivia. I just got rid of the llamas and put in stuff about kings having their heads chopped off. You have to bung in that kind of stuff, and then you just have to keep complaining about the weather and the crops and you can't go wrong, in peasant essays.'

Johnny lay on his bed reading *Only You Can Save Mankind.*

He could just about remember the days when you could still get games where the instructions consisted of

14

something that said, 'Press < for left and > for right and Fire for fire.'

But now you had to read a whole little book which was all about the game. It was really the manual, but they called it 'The Novel'.

Partly it was an anti-Wobbler thing. Someone in America or somewhere thought it was dead clever to make the game ask you little questions, like 'What's the first word on line 23 on page 19 of the manual?' and then reset the machine if you didn't answer them right, so they'd obviously never heard of Wobbler's dad's office's photocopier.

So there was this book. The ScreeWee had turned up out of nowhere and bombed some planets with humans on them. Nearly all the starships had been blown up. So there was only this one left, the experimental one. It was all that stood against the ScreeWee hordes. And only *you* . . . that is to say John Maxwell, aged twelve, in between the time you get home from school and get something to eat and do your homework . . . can save mankind.

Nowhere did it say what you were supposed to do if the ScreeWee hordes didn't want to fight.

He switched on the computer, and pressed the Load Game key.

There was the ship again, right in the middle of his sights.

He picked up the joystick thoughtfully.

There was an immediate message on the screen. Well, not exactly a message. More a picture. Half a dozen little egg-shaped blobs, with tails. They didn't move.

What kind of message is that? he thought.

Perhaps there was a special message he ought to

send. 'Die, Creep' didn't seem to fit properly at the moment.

He typed: Whats hpaening?

Immediately a reply appeared on the screen, in yellow letters.

We surrender. Do not shoot. See, we show you pictures of our children.

He typed: Is this a trick WObbler?

It took a little while before the reply came.

Am not trick wobbler. We give in. No more war.

Johnny thought for a while, and then typed: Youre not supoosed to give ni.

Want to go home.

Johnny typed: It says in the book you blue up a lot of planets.

Lies!

Johnny stared at the screen. What he wanted to type was: No, I mean, this cant happen, youre Aliens, you cant not want to be shot at, no other game aliens have ever stopped aliening across the screen, they never said We DonT Want to Go.

And then he thought: they never had the chance. *They* couldn't.

But games are a lot better now.

They never made things like the old MegaZoids seem *real*, with stories about them and Full-Colour Graphics.

This is probably that Virtual Reality they're always talking about on the television.

He typed: It is only a game, after all.

What is a game?

He typed: Who ARE you?

The screen flickered. Something a bit like a newt but more like an alligator looked back at him.

16

I am the Captain, said the yellow letters. *Do not shoot!*

Johnny typed: I shoot at you and you shoto at me. That is the game.

But we die.

Johnny typed: Sometimes I die. I die a lot.

But YOU live again.

Johnny stared at the words for a moment. Then he typed: Dont you?

No. How could this be? When we die, we die. For ever.

Johnny typed desperately: No, thats not right because, in the first mission, theres three ships you have to blow up before the first planet. I@ve played it lots of times and there@s always three ships there—

Different ships.

Johnny thought for a while and then typed: What happens if I switch of tthe machine?

We do not understand the question.

This is daft, thought Johnny. It's just a very unusual game. It's a special mission or something.

He typed: Why should I trust you?

LOOK BEHIND YOU.

Johnny sat bolt upright in his chair. Then he let himself swivel around, very cautiously.

Of course, there was no-one there. Why should there be anyone there? It was a *game*.

The newt face had disappeared from the screen, leaving the familiar picture of the inside of the starfighter. And there was the radar screen—

—covered in yellow dots.

Yellow for the enemy.

Johnny picked up the joystick and turned the starfighter around. The entire ScreeWee fleet was there. Ship after ship was hanging in space behind him.

Little fighters, big cruisers, massive battleships.

If they all had him in their sights, and if they fired . . .

He didn't want to die.

Hang on, hang on. You don't die. You just play the game again.

This was *nuts*. It was time to stop it.

He typed: All right what happens now?

We want to go home.

He typed: All right no problem.

You give us safe conduct.

He typed: OK yes.

The screen went blank.

And that was it? No music? No 'Congratulations, You've Got the Highest Score'?

Just the little prompt, flashing on and off.

What did safe conduct mean, anyway?

2

Operate Controls To Play Game

You never said to your parents, 'Hey, I really need a computer because that way I can play *Megasteroids*.'

No, you said, 'I really need a computer because of school.'

It's *educational*.

Anyway, there had to be a good side to the Trying Times everyone was going through in this house. If you hung around in your room and generally kept your head down, stuff like computers sort of happened. It made everyone feel better.

And it *was* quite useful for school sometimes. Johnny had written 'What it felt like to be different sorts of peasants' on it, and printed them out on the printer, although he had to rewrite them in his handwriting because although the school taught Keyboard Skills and New Technology you got into trouble if you used keyboard skills and new technology actually to do anything.

Funnily enough, it wasn't much good for maths. He'd always had trouble with algebra, because they wouldn't let you get away with 'What it feels like to be x^2'. But he had an arrangement with Bigmac about that, because Bigmac got the same feeling when he looked at an essay project as Johnny did when he was faced with a quadratic equation. Anyway, it didn't matter that much. If you kept your head down, they were generally so grateful that you were not, e.g., causing policemen to come to the school, or actually nailing a teacher to anything, that you got left alone.

But mainly the computer was good for games. If you turned the volume control up, you didn't have to hear the shouting.

The ScreeWee mother ship was in uproar. There was still a haze of smoke in the air from the last bombardment, and indistinct figures pattered back and forth, trying to fix things up well enough to survive the journey.

The Captain sat back in her chair on the huge, shadowy bridge. She was yellow under the eyes, a sure sign of lack of sleep. So much to be done . . . half the fighters were damaged, and the main ships were in none too good condition, and there was hardly any room and certainly no food for all the survivors they were taking on board.

She looked up. There was the Gunnery Officer.

'This is not a wise move,' he said.

'It is the only one I have,' said the Captain wearily.

'No! We must fight on!'

'And then we die,' said the Captain. 'We fight, and then we die. That's how it goes.'

'Then we die gloriously!'

'There's an important word in that sentence,' said the Captain. 'And it's not the word "gloriously".'

The Gunnery Officer went light green with rage.

'He's attacked hundreds of our ships!'

'And then he stopped.'

'None of the others have,' said the Gunnery Officer. 'They're *humans*! You can't trust a *human*. They shoot *everything*.'

The Captain rested her snout on one hand.

'He doesn't,' she said. 'He listened. He talked. None of the others did. He may be the One.'

The Gunnery Officer placed his upper two front hands on the desk and glared at her.

'Well,' he said, '*I've* talked to the other officers. I don't believe in legends. When the full enormity of what you have done is understood, you will be relieved of your command!'

She turned tired eyes towards him.

'Good,' she said. 'But right now, I *am* Captain. I am *responsible*. Do you understand? Have you got the faintest idea of what that *means*? Now . . . *go!*'

He didn't like it, but he couldn't disobey. I can have him shot, she thought. It'd be a good idea. Bound to save trouble later on. It'll be No. 235 on the list of Things to Do . . .

She turned back to continue staring at the stars outside, on the huge screen that filled one wall.

The enemy ship still hung there.

What kind of person is it? she thought. Despicable though they are, there's so few of them. But they keep coming back! What's their secret?

But you can be sure of one thing. They surely only send their bravest and their best.

The advantage of the Trying Times was that helping yourself from the fridge was OK. There didn't seem to be any proper mealtimes any more in any case. Or any real cooking.

Johnny made himself spaghetti and baked beans.

There was no sound from the living-room, although the TV was on.

Then he watched a bit of television in his room. He'd been given the old one when they got the new one. It wasn't very big and you had to get up and walk over to it every time you wanted to change channels or the volume or whatever, but these were Trying Times.

There was a film on the News showing some missiles streaking over some city. It was quite good.

Then he went to bed.

He was not entirely surprised to wake up at the controls of a starfighter.

It had been like that with *Captain Zoom*. You couldn't get it out of your head. After an evening's concentrated playing you were climbing ladders and dodging laser-zap bolts all night.

It was a pretty good dream, even so. He could *feel* the seat under him. And the cabin smelled of hot oil and overheated plastic and unwashed people.

It *looked* pretty much like the one he saw on the screen every evening, except that there was a thin film of grease and dirt over everything. But there was the radar screen, and the weapons console, and the joystick . . .

Hey, *much* better than the computer! The cabin was full of noises – the click and whirr of fans, the hum and buzz of instruments.

And better graphics. You get much better graphics in your dreams.

The ScreeWee fleet hung in the ai— hung in space in front of him.

Wow!

Although dreams ought to be a bit more exciting.

You got chased in dreams. Things *happened* to you. Sitting in the cockpit of a starfighter bristling with weapons was fun, but things ought to *happen* . . .

He wondered if he should launch a missile or something . . . No, hang on, they'd surrendered. And there was that thing about safe conduct.

His hands wandered over the switches in front of him. They were a bit different from the computer keyboard, but *this* one—

'*Are you receiving me?*'

The face of the Captain appeared on the communications screen.

'Yes?' said Johnny.

'*We are ready.*'

'Ready?' said Johnny. 'What for?'

'*Lead the way,*' said the Captain. The voice came out of a grille beside the screen. It must be being translated by something, Johnny thought. I shouldn't think giant newts speak English.

'Where to?' he said. 'Where are we going?'

'*Earth.*'

'Earth? Hang on! That's where *I* live! People can get into serious trouble showing huge alien fleets where they live!'

The grille hummed and buzzed for a while. Then the Captain said: '*Apology. That is a direct translation. We call the planet that is our home, "Earth". When I speak in ScreeWee, your computer finds the word in your language that means the same thing. The actual word in ScreeWee sounds like . . .*' There was a noise like someone taking their foot out of a wet cowpat. '*I will show our home to you.*'

A red circle suddenly developed on the navigation screen.

Johnny knew about that. You just moved a green circle over it, the computer went *binkabinkabinka*, and you'd set your course.

They've shown me where they live.

The thought sunk in.

They trust me.

As he moved his fighter forwards, the entire alien fleet pulled in behind him. They eclipsed the stars.

The cabin hummed and buzzed quietly to itself.

Well, at least it didn't look too hard . . .

A green dot appeared ahead of him.

He watched it get bigger, and recognized the shape of a starfighter, just like his.

But it was a little hard to make it out.

This was because it was half-hidden by laser bolts.

It was firing at him as it came.

And it was travelling so fast it was very nearly catching up with its own fire.

Johnny jerked the joystick and his ship rolled out of the way as the . . . the *enemy* starfighter roared past and barrelled on towards the ScreeWee ships.

The whole sky full of ScreeWee ships.

Which had surrendered to *him*.

But people out there were still playing the game.

'No! Listen to me! They're not fighting any more!'

The starfighter turned in a wide curve and headed directly for the command ship. Johnny saw it launch a missile. Someone sitting at a keyboard somewhere had launched a missile.

'*Listen!* You've got to *stop*!'

It's not listening to me, he thought. You don't listen to the enemy. The enemy's there to be shot at. That's why it's the enemy. That's what the enemy's *for*.

He swung around to follow the starship, which had

slowed down. It was pouring shot after shot into the command ship . . .

. . . which wasn't firing back.

Johnny stared in horror.

The ship rocked under the hail of fire. The Gunnery Officer crawled across the shaking floor and pulled himself up beside the Captain's chair.

'Fool! Fool! I told you this would happen! I demand that we return fire!'

The Captain was watching the Chosen One's ship. It hadn't moved.

'No,' she said. 'We have to give him a chance. We must not fire on human ships.'

'A *chance*? How much of a chance do *we* have? I shall give the order to—'

The Captain moved very fast. When her hand stopped she was holding a gun very close to the Gunnery Officer's head. It was really only a ceremonial weapon; normally ScreeWee fought only with their claws. But its shape said very clearly that things came out of the hole in the front end with the very definite purpose of travelling fast through the air and then killing people.

'No,' she said.

The Gunnery Officer's face went blue, a sure sign of terror. But he had enough courage left to say: 'You would not *dare* fire!'

It's a game, thought Johnny. There's not a *real* person in that ship. It's someone playing a game. It's *all* a game. It's just things happening on a screen somewhere.

No.

I mean, *yes*.

But . . .

. . . at the same time . . .

. . . it's all happening *here . . .*

His own ship leapt forward.

It was easy. It was so easy. Just line up circles on the screen, *binkabinkabinka*, and then press the Fire button until every weapon on the ship was empty. He'd done it many times before.

The invader hadn't even seen him. It launched some missiles – and then blew up in an impressive display of graphics.

That's all it is, Johnny told himself. Just things on a screen. It's not real. There's no arms and feet spinning away through the wreckage. It's all a game.

The missiles arrived . . .

The whole cockpit went blinding white.

He was aware, just for a moment, of cold space around him, with things in it . . .

A bookcase. A chair. A bed.

He was sitting in front of the computer. The screen was blank. He was holding the joystick so hard that he had to concentrate to let go of it.

The clock by his bed said 6:3≡, because it was broken. But it meant he'd have to get up in another hour or so.

He sat with his quilt around him watching the television until the alarm went off.

There were some more pictures of missiles and bullets streaking over a city. They looked pretty much the same as the ones he'd seen last night, but were probably back by popular demand.

He felt sick.

*   *   *

26

Yo-less could help, Johnny decided.

He normally hung out with Wobbler and Bigmac on the bit of wall behind the school library. They weren't exactly a gang. If you take a big bag of crisps and shake them up, all the little bits end up in one corner.

Yo-less was called Yo-less because he never said 'Yo'. He'd given up objecting to the name by now. At least it was better than Nearly Crucial, which was the last nickname, and MC Spanner, which was the one before that. Johnny was the official nickname generator.

Yo-less said he'd never said 'crucial', either. He pointed out that Johnny was white and never said, 'YerWhat? YerWhat? YerWhat?' or 'Ars-nal! Ars-nal!' and anyway, you shouldn't make jokes about racial stereotyping.

Johnny didn't go into too much detail. He just talked about the dream, and not about the messages on the screen. Yo-less listened carefully. Yo-less listened to everything carefully. It worried teachers, the way he listened carefully to everything they said. They always suspected he was trying to catch them out.

He said, 'What you've got here is a projection of a psychological conflict. That's all. Want a cheese ring?'

'What's that?'

'It's just crunchy cheesy-flavoured—'

'I mean the other thing you said.'

Yo-less passed the packet on to Bigmac.

'Well . . . your mum and dad are splitting up, right? Well-known fact.'

'Could be. It's a bit of a trying time,' said Johnny.

'O-kay. And there's nothing you can do about it.'

'Shouldn't think so,' said Johnny.

'And this definitely affects you,' said Yo-less.

'I suppose so,' said Johnny cautiously. 'I know I have to do a lot of my own cooking.'

'Right. So you project your . . . um . . . suppressed emotions on to a computer game. Happens all the time,' said Yo-less, whose mother was a nurse, and who wanted to be a doctor if he grew up. 'You can't solve the *real* problems, so you turn them into problems you *can* solve. Like . . . if this was thirty years ago, you'd probably dream about fighting dragons or something. It's a projected fantasy.'

'Saving hundreds of intelligent newts doesn't sound very easy to solve,' said Johnny.

'Dunno,' said Bigmac, happily. 'Ratatatat-blam! No more problem.' Bigmac wore large boots and camouflage trousers all the time. You could spot him a mile off by his camouflage trousers.

'The thing is,' said Yo-less, 'it's not real. Real's real. But stuff on a screen isn't.'

'I've cracked *Stellar Smashers*,' said Wobbler. 'You can have that if you want. Everyone says it's a lot better.'

'No-oo,' said Johnny, 'I think I'll stick with this one for a while. See if I can get to level twenty-one.'

'If you get to level twenty-one and blow up the whole fleet you get a special number on the screen, and if you write off to Gobi Software you get a five pound token,' said Wobbler. 'It was in *Computer Weekly*.'

Johnny thought about the Captain.

'A whole five pounds?' he said. 'Gosh.'

It was Games in the afternoon. Bigmac was the only one who played. He'd never been keen until they'd introduced hockey. You got a club to hit people, he said.

Yo-less didn't do sport because of intellectual incompatibility. Wobbler didn't do sport because the sports master had asked him not to. Johnny didn't do sport because he had a permanent note, and no-one cared much anyway, so he went home early and spent the afternoon reading the manual.

He didn't touch the computer before tea.

There was an extended News, which meant that *Cobbers* was postponed. There were the same pictures of missiles streaking across a city that he'd seen the night before, except that now there were more journalists in sand-coloured shirts with lots of pockets talking excitedly about them.

He heard his mother downstairs complain about *Cobbers*, and by the sound of the raised voices that started Trying Times again.

There was some History homework about Christopher Columbus. He looked him up in the encyclopedia and copied out four hundred words, which usually worked. He drew a picture of Columbus as well, and coloured it in.

After a while he realized that he was putting off switching the computer on. It came to something, he thought, when you did school work rather than play games . . .

It wouldn't hurt to at least have a game of *Pac-Man* or something. Trouble was, the ghosts would probably stay in the middle of the screen and refuse to come out and be eaten. He didn't think he could cope with that. He'd got enough to worry about as it was.

On top of it all, his father came upstairs to be fatherly. This happened about once a fortnight. There didn't seem to be any way of stopping it. You had to put up with twenty minutes of being asked about how you were getting on at school, and had you *really* thought about what you wanted to be when you grew up.

The thing to do was not encourage things, but as politely as possible.

His father sat on the edge of the bed and looked around the room as though he'd never seen it before.

After the normal questions about teachers Johnny hadn't had since the first year, his father stared at nothing much for a while and then said, 'Things have been a bit tricky lately. I expect you've noticed.'

'No.'

'It's been a bit tricky at work. Not a good time to start a new business.'

'Yes.'

'Everything all right?'

'Yes.'

'Nothing you want to talk about?'

'No. I don't think so.'

His father looked around the room again. Then he said, 'Remember last year, when we all went down to Falmouth for the week?'

'Yes.'

'You enjoyed that, didn't you?'

He'd got sunburnt and twisted his ankle on some rocks and he had to get up at 8.30 *every morning*, even though it was supposed to be a holiday. And the only TV in the hotel was in front of some old woman who never let go of the remote-control.

'Yes.'

'We ought to go again.'

His father was staring at him.

'Yes,' said Johnny. 'That would be nice.'

'How're you getting on with *Space Invaders*?'

'Sorry?'

'*Space Invaders*. On the computer.'

Johnny turned to look at the blank screen.

'What're Space Invaders?' he said.

'Isn't that what they're called any more? Space Invaders? You used to get them in pubs and things, oh, before you were born. Rows of spiky triangular green aliens with six legs kept on coming down the screen and we had to shoot them.'

Johnny gave this some thought. 'What happened when you'd shot them all, then?'

'Oh, you got some more.' His father stood up. 'I expect it's all more complicated now, though.'

'Yes.'

'Done your homework, have you?'

'Yes.'

'What was it?'

'History. Had to write about Christopher Columbus.'

'Hmm? You could put in that he didn't set out to discover America. He was really looking for Asia and found America by accident.'

'Yes. It says that in the encyclopedia.'

'Glad to see you're using it.'

'Yes. It's very interesting.'

'Good. Right. Right, then. Well, I'm going to have another look at those accounts . . .'

'Right.'

'If there's anything you want to talk about, you know . . .'

'All right.'

Johnny waited until he heard the living-room door shut again. He wondered if he ought to have asked where the instruction manual for the dishwasher was.

He switched on the computer.

After a while, the screen for *Only You Can Save Mankind* came on. He watched the introductory bit moodily, and then picked up the joystick.

There weren't any aliens.

For a little while he thought he'd done something wrong. He started the game again.

There were still no aliens. All there was, was the blackness of space, sprinkled with a few twinkling stars.

He flew around until he was out of fuel.

No ScreeWee, no dots on the radar screen. No game.

They'd gone.

3

Cereal Killers

There was more news these days than normal. Half the time the TV was showing pictures of tanks and maps of deserts with green and red arrows all over them, while in the corner of the screen would be a photo of a journalist with a phone to his ear, talking in a crackly voice.

It crackled in the background while Johnny phoned up Wobbler.

'Yes?'

'Can I speak to Wob . . . to Stephen, please?'

Mutter, clonk, bump, scuffle.

'Yes?'

'It's me, Wobbler.'

'Yes?'

'Have you had a look at *Only You Can Save Mankind* lately?'

'No. Hey, listen, I've found a way to—'

'Could you have a go with it right now, please?'

Pause.

'You all right?'

'What?'

'You sound a bit weird.'

'Look, go and have a go with the game, will you?'

It was an hour before Wobbler phoned back. Johnny waited on the stairs.

'Can I speak—'

'It's me.'

'There's no aliens, right?'

'Yes!'

'Probably something built into the game. You can do that, you know. A kind of time bomb thing. Maybe it's programmed to make all the aliens vanish on a certain date.'

'What for?'

'Make things more interesting, I expect. Probably Gobi Software will be putting adverts in the computer papers about it. You all right? Your voice sounds a bit squeaky.'

'No problem.'

'You coming down to the mall tomorrow?'

'Yeah.'

'See you, then. Chow.'

Johnny stared at the dead phone. Of course, there *were* things like that on computers. There'd been something in the papers about it. A Friday the 13th virus, or something. Something in the program kept an eye on the date, and when it was Friday the 13th it was supposed to do something nasty to computers all over the country.

There had been stories about Evil Computer Hackers Menacing Society, and Wobbler had come to school in home-made dark glasses for a week.

Johnny went back and watched the screen for a while. Stars occasionally went past.

Wobbler had written an actual computer game like this once. It was called *Journey to Alpha Centauri*. It was a screen with some dots on it. Because, he said, it happened in *real time*, which no-one had ever heard of until computers. He'd seen on TV that it took three thousand years to get to Alpha Centauri. He had written it so that if anyone kept their computer on for three thousand years, they'd be rewarded by a little dot appearing in the middle of the screen, and then a message saying, 'Welcome to Alpha Centauri. Now go home.'

Johnny watched the screen for a bit longer. Once or twice he nudged the joystick, to go on a different course. It didn't make much difference. Space looked the same from every direction.

'Hello? Anybody there?' he whispered.

He watched some television before he went to bed. There were some more missiles, and someone going on about some other missiles which were supposed to knock down the first type of missile.

The fleet travelled in the shape of a giant cone, hundreds of miles long. The Captain looked back at it. There were scores of mother ships, hundreds of fighters. More and more kept joining them as news of the surrender spread.

The Chosen One's ship flew a little way ahead of the fleet. It wasn't answering messages.

But no-one was shooting at them. There hadn't been a human ship visible for hours. Perhaps, the Captain thought, it's really working. We're leaving them behind . . .

Johnny woke up in the game.

It was hard to sleep in the starship. The seat started out as the most comfortable thing in the whole world, but it was amazing how uncomfortable it became after a few hours. And the lavatory was a complicated arrangement of tubes and trapdoors and it wasn't, he was beginning to notice, entirely smellproof.

That's what the computer games couldn't give you: the *smell* of space. It had its own kind of smell, like a machine's armpit. You didn't get dirty, because there was no dirt, but there was a sort of grimy cleanliness about everything.

The radar went *ping*.

After a while, he could see a dot ahead of him. It wasn't moving much, and it certainly wasn't firing.

He left the fleet and went to investigate.

It was a huge ship. Or, at least, it had been once. Quite a lot of it had been melted off.

It drifted along, absolutely dead, tumbling very gently. It was green, and vaguely triangular, except for six legs, or possibly arms. Three of them were broken stubs. It looked like a cross between a spider and an octopus, designed by a computer and made out of hundreds of cubes, bolted together.

As the giant hulk turned he could see huge gashes in it, with melted edges. There was a suggestion of floors inside.

He switched on the radio.

'Captain?'

'Yes?'

'Can you see this thing here? What is it?'

'We find them sometimes. We think they belonged to an ancient race, now extinct. We don't know what they called themselves, or where they came from. The ships are very crude.'

The dead ship turned slowly. There was another long burn down the other side.

'I think they were called Space Invaders,' said Johnny.

'The human name for them?'

'Yes.'

'I thought so.'

Johnny was glad he couldn't see the Captain's face.

He thought: No-one knows where they came from, or even what they called themselves. And now no-one ever will.

The radar went *ping* again.

There was a human ship heading towards the fleet, at high speed.

This time, he didn't hesitate.

The point was, the ScreeWee weren't very *good* at fighting. After the first few games it was quite easy to beat them. They couldn't seem to get the hang of it. They didn't know how to be sneaky, or when to dodge.

It was the same with all of them, come to think of it. Johnny had played lots of games with words like 'Space' and 'Battle' and 'Cosmic' in the titles, and all the aliens were the sort you could beat after a few weeks' playing.

This player didn't stand a chance against a real human.

You got six missiles. Johnny had two streaking away before the enemy was much larger than a dot. Then he just kept his finger on the Fire button until there was nothing left to fire.

A spreading cloud of wreckage, and that was it.

It wasn't as if anyone would die, after all. Whoever had been in there would just have to start the game again.

It *felt* real, but that was just the dream . . .

Dreams always felt real.

He turned his attention to the thing by the control

chair. It had a nozzle which filled a paper cup with something like thin vegetable soup, and a slot which pushed out very large plastic bags containing very small things like sandwiches. The bags had to be big to get all the list of additives on. They contained absolutely everything necessary to keep a star warrior healthy. Not happy, but healthy . . .

He'd taken one mouthful when something slammed into the ship. A red glare filled the cabin; alarms started to blare.

He looked up in time to see a ship curving away for another run.

He hadn't even glanced at the radar.

He'd been eating his *tea*!

He spun the ship. The multi-vitamin sandwich flew around into the wiring somewhere.

It was coming back to get him. He prodded furiously at the control panel.

Hang on . . .

What was the worst that could happen to him?

He could wake up in bed.

He took his time. He dodged. He weaved. Another missile hit the ship. As the attacker roared past, Johnny fired, with everything.

Another cloud of wreckage.

No problem.

But it must have fired a missile just before he got it. There was another red flash. The lights went out. The ship jumped. His head bounced off the seatback and banged on to the control panel.

He opened his eyes.

Right. And you wake up back in your bedroom.

A light winked at him.

There was something beeping.

Bound to be the alarm clock. That's how dreams end . . .

He lifted his head. The flashing light was oblong. He tried to focus.

There were shapes there.

But they weren't saying 6:3≡.

They were spelling out 'AIR LEAK', and behind the insistent beeping was a terrible hissing sound.

No, no, he thought. This doesn't happen.

He pushed himself up. There were lots of red lights. He pressed some buttons hurriedly, but this had no effect at all except to make some more lights go red.

He didn't know much about the controls of a star-ship, other than fast, slow, left, right and fire, but there were whole rows of flashing alarms which suggested that a lot of things he didn't know about were going wrong. He stared at some red letters which said 'SECONDARY PUMPS FAILURE'. He didn't know what the secondary pumps were, either, but he wished, he really wished, they hadn't failed.

His head ached. He reached up, and there was real blood on his hand. And he knew that he was going to die. Really die.

No, he thought. Please! I'm John Maxwell. Please! I'm twelve. I'm not dying in a spaceshi—

The beeping got louder.

He looked at the sign again.

It was flashing 6:3≡.

About time, he thought, as he passed out . . .

And woke up.

He was at the computer again. It wasn't switched on, and he was freezing cold.

He had a headache, but a tentative feel said there was no blood. It was *just* a headache.

He stared into the dark black screen, and wondered what it felt like to be a ScreeWee.

It felt like that, except that you didn't wake up. It was always AIR LEAK, or *Alert*Alert*Alert* beeping on and off, and then perhaps the freezing cold of space, and then nothing.

He had breakfast.

You got a free alien in every pack of sugar-glazed Snappiflakes. It was a new thing. Or an old thing, being tried again.

The one that ended up in his bowl was orange and had three eyes and four arms. And it was holding a ray gun in each hand.

His father hadn't got up. His mother was watching the little television in the kitchen, where a very large man disguised as an entire desert was pointing to a lot of red and blue arrows on a map.

He went down to Neil Armstrong Mall.

He took the plastic alien with him. That'd be the way to invade a planet. One alien in every box! Wait until they were in every cupboard in the country, send out the signal and *bazaam!*

Cereal killers!

Maybe on some other planet somewhere you got a free human in every packet of ammonia-coated Snappicrystals. Hey, *zorks!* Collect the Whole Set! And there'd be all these little plastic people. Holding guns, of course. You just had to walk down the street to see that, of course, everyone had a gun.

He looked out of the bus window.

That was it, really. No-one would bother to put plastic aliens inside the plastic cereal if they were just,

40

you know, doing everyday things. Holding the Cosmiczippo Ray™ hedge clippers! Getting on the Megadeath™ bus! Hanging out at the Star Thruster Mall!

The trouble with all the aliens he'd seen was that they either wanted to eat you or play music at you until you became better people. You never got the sort that just wanted to do something ordinary like borrow the lawn mower.

Wobbler and Yo-less and Bigmac were trying to hang out by the ornamental fountain, but really they were just hanging around. Yo-less was wearing the same grey trousers he wore to school. You couldn't hang out in grey trousers. And Wobbler still wore his sunglasses, except they weren't real sunglasses because he had to wear ordinary glasses *anyway*; they were those clip-on sunglasses for tourists. Also, they weren't the same size as the glasses underneath, and had rubbed red marks on his nose. And he wore an anorak. Wobbler was probably the only person in the universe who still wore an anorak. And Bigmac, in addition to his camouflage trousers and 'Terminator' T-shirt with 'Blackbury Skins' on the back in biro, had got hold of a belt made entirely of cartridge cases. He looked stupid.

'Yo, duds,' said Johnny.

'We've been here ages,' said Yo-less.

'I went one stop past on the bus and had to walk back,' said Johnny. 'Thinking about other things. What's happening?'

'Do you mean what's happening, or sort of hey, my man, what's *happening*?' said Wobbler.

'What's happening?' said Johnny.

'I want to go into J&J Software,' said Wobbler. 'They might have got *Cosmic Coffee Mats* in. It got a review in *Bazzammm!* and they said it's got an unbreakable copy protection.'

'Did they say it was any good?' said Bigmac.

'Who cares?'

'You'll get caught one day,' said Yo-less.

'Then you get given a job in Silicon Valley, designing antipiracy software,' said Wobbler. Behind his two thicknesses of glasses, his eyes lit up. Wobbler thought that California was where good people went when they died.

'No, you don't. You just get in trouble and you get sued,' said Yo-less. 'And the police take all your computers away. There was something in the paper.'

They wandered aimlessly towards the computer shop.

'I saw this film once, right, where there were these computer games and if you were really good the aliens came and got you and you had to fly a spaceship and fight a whole bad alien fleet,' said Bigmac.

'Did you beat it? I mean, in the film, the alien fleet got beaten?'

Bigmac gave Johnny an odd look.

'Of *course*. Sure. There wouldn't be any point otherwise, would there.'

'Only you can save mankind,' said Johnny.

'What?'

'It's the game,' said Wobbler.

'But it *always* says something like that on the boxes you get games in,' said Johnny. Except if you get them from Wobbler, he added to himself, when you just get a disc.

'Well. Yeah. Something like that. Why not?'

'I mean they never say, "Only You are going to be put inside a Billion Pounds Worth of Machine with more Switches that you've Ever Seen and be Blown to Bits by a Thousand Skilled Enemy Pilots because You Don't Really Know how to Fly It." '

They wandered past Mr Zippy's Ice Cream Extravaganza.

'Can't see that catching on,' said Wobbler. 'Can't see them ever selling a game called *Get Shot to Pieces*.'

'You still having trouble at home?' said Yo-less.

'It's all gone quiet,' said Johnny.

'That can be worse than shouting.'

'Yes.'

'It's not that bad when your mum and dad split up,' said Wobbler, 'although you get to see more museums than is good for you.'

'Still found no aliens?' said Yo-less.

'Um. Not in the game.'

'Still dreaming about them?' said Wobbler.

'Sort of.'

Someone handing out leaflets about Big Savings on Double Glazing gave one, in desperation, to Yo-less. He took it gravely, thanked them, folded it in two and put it in his pocket. Yo-less always filed this sort of thing. You never knew when it might come in handy, he said. One day he might want to doubleglaze his surgery, and he'd be in a good position to compare offers.

'Anyone see the war on the box last night?' said Bigmac. 'Way to go, eh?'

'Way to go where?' said Yo-less.

'We're really kicking some butt!'

'Some but what?' said Wobbler.

'We'll give them the "Mother-in-law of All Battles", eh?' said Bigmac, still trying to stir some patriotism.

'Nah. It's not like real fighting,' said Wobbler. 'It's just TV fighting.'

43

'Wish I was in the army,' said Bigmac, wistfully. 'Blam!' He shot the double-glazing lady, who didn't notice. Bigmac had a habit of firing imaginary guns. Other people played air guitar, he shot air rifles.

'Couple more years,' he said. 'That's all.'

'You ought to write to Stormin' Norman,' said Wobbler. 'Ask him to keep the war going until you get there.'

'He's done pretty well for someone called Norman,' said Yo-less. 'I mean . . . Norman? Not very mackko, is it? It's like Bruce, or Rodney.'

'He had to be Norman,' said Wobbler, 'otherwise he couldn't be Stormin'. You couldn't have Stormin' Bruce. Come on.'

J&J Software was always packed on a Saturday morning. There were always a couple of computers running games, and always a cluster of people gathered round them. No-one knew who J&J were, since the shop was run by Mr Patel, who had eyes like a hawk. He always watched Wobbler very carefully, on the fairly accurate basis that Wobbler distributed more games than he did and didn't even charge anyone for them.

The four of them split up. Bigmac wasn't much interested in games, and Yo-less went down to look at the videos. Wobbler had found someone who knew even more complicated stuff about computers than he did himself.

Johnny mooched along the racks of games.

I wonder if the ScreeWee do this, he thought. Or people on Jupiter or somewhere. Go down to a shop and buy 'Shoot the Human' games. And have films where there's a human running around the place terrorizing a spaceship—

He became aware of a raised voice at the counter.

You didn't often get girls in J&J Software. Once, quite a long time ago, during a bit of time she'd set aside for parenting, Johnny's mother had tried playing a game. It had been quite a simple one – you had to shoot asteroids and flying saucers and things. It had been embarrassing. It had been amazing that the flying saucers had even bothered to shoot back. More likely they should have parked and all the aliens could have looked out of the windows and made rude noises. Women didn't have a clue.

A girl was complaining to Mr Patel about a game she'd bought. Everyone knew you couldn't do that, even if you'd opened the box and it was full of nothing but mouse droppings. Mr Patel took the view that once the transparent wrapper had come off, even the Pope wouldn't be allowed to return a game, not even if he got God to come in as well. This was because he'd met people like Wobbler before.

The boys watched in fascinated horror.

She kept tapping the offending box with a finger.

'*And* who wants to see nothing but stars?' she said. 'I've seen stars before, *actually*. It says on the box that you fight dozens of different kinds of alien ships. There isn't even *one*.'

Mr Patel muttered something. Johnny wasn't close enough to hear. But the girl's voice had a kind of penetrating quality, like a corkscrew. When she spoke in italics, you could *hear* them.

'Oh, no. You can't say that. Because how can I tell if it works without *trying* it? That comes under the Sale of Goods Act (1983).'

The awed watchers were astonished to see a slightly hunted look in Mr Patel's eyes. Up until now he'd never met anyone who could pronounce brackets.

He muttered something else.

'Copy it? Why should I copy it? I've *bought* it. It says on the box you meet fascinating alien races. Well, all I got was one ship and some stupid message on the screen and then it ran away. I don't call that fascinating alien races.'

Message . . .

Ran away . . .

Johnny sidled closer.

Mr Patel muttered something else, and then turned to one of the shelves. The shop watched in amazement. There was a *new* game in his hand. He was actually going to make an exchange. This was like Genghis Khan deciding not to attack a city but stay at home and watch the football instead.

Then he held up his hand, nodded at the girl, and stalked over to one of the shop's own computers, the ones with so many fingermarks on the keys that you couldn't read them any more.

Everyone watched in silence as he loaded up the copy of the game that the girl had brought back. The music came on. The title scrolled up the screen, like the one in Star Wars. It was the usual stuff: 'The mighty ScreeWee fleet have attacked the Federation,' whatever that was, 'and only *you* . . .'

And then there was space. It was computer space – a sort of black, with the occasional star rolling past.

'There ought to be six ships on the first mission,' said someone behind Johnny.

Mr Patel scowled at him. He pressed a key cautiously.

'You've just fired a torpedo at nothing, Mr Patel,' said Wobbler.

Finally Mr Patel gave up. He waved his hands in the air.

'How d'you find the things to shoot?' he said.

'They find you,' said someone. 'You should be dead by now.'

'See?' said the girl. 'You get nothing but space. I left it on for hours, and there was just space.'

'Maybe you're not persevering. You kids don't know the meaning of the word persevere,' said Mr Patel.

Wobbler looked over the shopkeeper's head to Johnny and raised his eyebrows.

'It's like persistently trying,' said Johnny helpfully.

'Oh. Right. Well, I persistently tried the other night and *I* didn't find any, either.'

Mr Patel carefully unwrapped the new copy of the game. The shop watched as he slotted the disc into the computer.

'Then let us see what the game looks like before Mr Wobbler plays his little tricks,' he said.

There was the title screen. There was the story, such as it was. And the instructions.

And space.

'Soon we shall see,' said Mr Patel.

And then more space.

'This one was only delivered yesterday.'

Lots more space. That was the thing about space.

Mr Patel picked up the box and looked at it carefully, But they'd all seen him take off the polythene.

They've gone, thought Johnny.

Even on the new games.

They've all gone.

People were laughing. But Wobbler and Yo-less were staring at him.

47

4

'No-one Really Dies'

'I reckon,' said Bigmac, 'I *reckon* . . .'

'Yes?' said Yo-less.

'I reckon . . . Ronald McDonald is like Jesus Christ.'

Bigmac did that kind of thing. Sometimes he came out with the kind of big, slow statement that suggested some sort of deep thinking had been going on for some time. It was like mountains. Johnny knew they were made by continents banging together, but no-one ever saw it happening.

'Yes?' said Yo-less, in a kind voice. 'And why do you think this?'

'Well, look at all the advertising,' said Bigmac, waving a fry in the general direction of the rest of the burger bar. 'There's this happy land you go to where there's lakes of banana milkshake and – and trees covered in fries. And . . . and then there's the Hamburglar. He's the Devil.'

'Mr Zippy's advertised by a giant talking ice cream,' said Wobbler.

'I don't like that,' said Yo-less. 'I wouldn't trust an ice cream that's trying to get you to eat ice creams.'

Occasionally they talked like this for hours, when there was something they didn't want to talk about. But now they seemed to have run out of things to say.

They all looked silently at Johnny, who'd hardly touched his burger.

'Look, I don't *know* what's happening,' he said.

'Gobi Software're going to be really pissed off when they find out what you've done,' said Wobbler, grinning.

'I didn't do anything!' said Johnny. 'It's not my fault!'

'Could be a virus,' said Yo-less.

'Nah,' said Wobbler. 'I've got loads of viruses. They just muck up the computer. They don't muck up your head.'

'They could do,' said Yo-less. 'With flashing lights and stuff. Kind of like hypnosis.'

'You said before I was making it all up! *You* said I was projecting fantasies!'

'That was before old Patel went through half a dozen boxes. I'm glad I saw that. You know she actually got another copy *and* her money back, *actually*?'

Johnny smiled uncomfortably.

Wobbler drummed his fingers on the table, or partly on the table and partly in a pool of barbecue sauce.

'No, I still reckon it's just something Gobi Software did to all the games. Cor, I like the virus idea, though,' he said. 'Humans catching viruses off of computers? Nice one.'

'It's not like that,' said Johnny.

'They used to do this thing with films where they'd put in just one frame of something, like an ice cream or something, and it'd enter people's brains without them knowing it and they'd all want ice cream,' said Yo-less. 'Subliminal advertising, it was called. That'd be quite easy to do on a computer.'

Johnny thought about the Captain showing him

pictures of her children. That didn't sound like hypnosis. He didn't know what it *did* sound like, but it didn't sound like hypnosis.

'Perhaps they're real aliens and they're in control of your computer,' said Yo-less.

'OOOO – eee – OOO,' said Bigmac, waving his hands in the air and speaking in a hollow voice. 'Johnny Maxwell did not know it, but he had just strayed into . . . the Toilet Zone . . . deedledeedle, deedledeedle, deedledeedle . . .'

'After all, you're supposed to be leading them to Earth,' Yo-less went on.

'But that's just their own name for their own world,' said Johnny.

'You've only got their word for it. And they're newts, too. You could be bringing them *here*.'

They all looked up, in case they could see through the ceiling, T&F Insurance Services and the roof to a huge alien fleet in the sky above.

'You're just getting carried away,' said Wobbler. 'You can't invade a planet with a lot of aliens out of a computer game. They live on a screen. They're not *real*.'

'What're you going to do about it, anyway?' said Yo-less.

'Just keep doing it, I suppose,' said Johnny. 'Who was that girl in Patel's?'

'Don't know,' said Wobbler. 'Saw her in there once before playing *Cosmic Trek*. Girls aren't much good at computer games because they haven't got such a good grasp of spatial . . . something or other like we have,' he went on airily. 'You know. They can't think in three dimensions, or something. They haven't got the instincts for it.'

'The Captain's a female,' said Johnny.

'It's probably different for giant alligators,' said Wobbler.

Bigmac sucked a sachet of tomato ketchup.

'Do you think IT might still be going when I'm old enough to join the army?' he said, thoughtfully.

'No,' said Yo-less. 'Stormin' Bruce'll get it all sorted out. He'll kick some butt.'

They chorused 'Some but what?' like tired monks.

They went to the cinema in the afternoon. *Alabama Smith and the Emperor's Crown* was showing on Screen S. Wobbler said it was racist, but Yo-less said he quite enjoyed it. They discussed whether it could still be racist if Yo-less enjoyed it. Johnny bought popcorn all round. That was another thing about Trying Times – pocket money was erratic, but you tended to get more of it.

He had spaghetti hoops when he got home, and watched TV for a while. The pyramid-shaped man disguised as a desert seemed to be on a lot now. He told jokes sometimes. The journalists laughed a bit. Johnny quite liked Stormin' Norman. He looked the sort of man who could talk to the Captain.

Then there was a programme about saving whales. They thought it was a good idea.

Then you could win lots of money if you could put up with the game show's host and not, for example, choke him with a cuddly toy and run away.

There was the News. The walking desert again, and pictures of bombs being dropped down enemy chimneys with pin-point precision. And Sport.

And then . . .

All right. Let's see.

He switched on.

Yes. Space. And more space.

No ScreeWee anywhere.

Hang on, he thought. They're all in the big fleet, aren't they. Following me. They followed me out of – out of – out of *game* space. You must be able to get there from here, if you keep going long enough. In the right direction, too.

Which way did I go?

Can I catch myself up?

Can anyone *else* catch me up?

He watched the screen for a while. It was even more boring than the quiz show.

Sooner or later he'd have to go to sleep. He'd thought hard about this, while Alabama Smith was being chased by bad guys through a native market-place . . .

. . . Johnny had a theory about these market-places. Every spy film and every adventure had a chase through the native market-place, with lots of humorous rickshaws crashing into stalls and tables being knocked over and chickens squawking, and the theory was: it was the same market-place every time. It always *looked* the same. There was probably a stallholder somewhere who was getting very fed up with it . . .

Anyway . . .

He'd take his camera.

He went to bed early with the camera strap wound around his wrist. Cameras didn't dream.

The ship smelled *human*.

There were no alarms, no hissing noises.

I'm back, thought Johnny.

And there was the ScreeWee fleet, spread out across the sky behind him.

And the camera, with its strap wrapped around his

arm. He untangled it quickly and took a photo of the fleet. It whirred out of the machine after a few seconds. He held it under his armpit for a moment, and it gradually faded up. Yep. The fleet. If he could get it back, he'd have proof . . .

There was a red light flashing beside the screen on the console. Someone wanted to talk to him. He flicked the switch.

'We saw your ship explode,' came the voice of the Captain. The screen crackled for a moment, and then showed her face. It looked concerned. *'And then it . . . returned again. You are alive?'*

'Yes,' said Johnny, and then added, 'I think so.'

'Excuse me. I must ask. What happens to you?'

'What?'

'When you . . . go.'

Johnny thought: What do I tell her? I stay awake in school. I stay in my room a lot. I hang out with Wobbler and the others. We hang around in the mall, or in the park, or in one another's houses, although not my house at the moment because of Trying Times, and say things like 'I'm totally splanked' even though we're not sure what they mean. Sometimes we go to the cinema. We live in Blackbury, most excellent city of cool.

I must have the most boring life in the entire universe. I expect there's blobs living under rocks on Neptune that have a more interesting life than me . . .

'It'd be too hard to explain,' he said. 'I—'

There was a *ping* from the radar.

'I have to go,' he said, feeling a bit relieved. Facing someone else in mortal combat was better than trying to tell a giant newt about Trying Times.

There was a ship coming in fast. It didn't seem to

notice him. Its screen must be full of ScreeWee ships.

It was in the middle of his targeting grid. Around him, the starship hummed. He could feel the power under his thumb. Press the button and a million volts or amps or something of white-hot laser power would crackle out and—

His thumb trembled.

It didn't seem to want to move.

But no-one dies! he told himself. There's just someone somewhere sitting in their room in front of a computer! That's what it looks like to them! It's all just something on a screen! No-one really dies!

I can fire right into his retro-tubes with pin-point precision!

No-one really dies!

The ship roared past him and onwards, towards the fleet.

On the radar screen he saw two white dots, which meant that it had fired a couple of missiles. They streaked towards one of the smaller ScreeWee ships, with the attacker close behind them, firing as he went.

The ScreeWee burst into flame. Johnny knew you shouldn't be able to hear sound in space, but he did hear it – a long, low rumble, washing across the stars.

The human ship turned in a long curve and came back for another run.

The Captain's face appeared on the screen.

'We have surrendered! This must not be allowed!'

'I'm sorry, I—'

'You must stop this now!'

Johnny let his own ship accelerate while he tried to adjust the microphone.

'Game player! Game player! Stop now! Stop now or—'

Or what, he thought – or I'll shout 'stop' again?

He raised his thumb over the Fire button, took aim at the intruder—

'Please! I mean it!'

It was plunging on towards another ship, taking no notice of him.

'All right, then—'

Blinding blue light flashed across his vision. He shut his eyes and still the light was there, purple in the darkness. When he opened them again the ship ahead of him was just an expanding cloud of glittering dust.

He turned in his seat. The Captain's ship was right behind him. He could see its guns glowing.

They never did this in the game. They had much more firepower than you, but they used it stupidly. It had to be like that. You could only win against hundreds of alien ships if they had the same grasp of gunnery techniques as the common cucumber.

This time, every gun had fired at exactly the same time.

The Captain's face appeared on the screen.

I am sorry.

'What? What happened?'

It will not happen again, I promise you.

'What *happened*?'

There was silence. The Captain appeared to be looking at something beyond the camera range.

There was an unauthorized firing, she said. *Those responsible will be dealt with.*

'I was going after that ship,' said Johnny, uncertainly.

Yes. It is to be hoped that another time you can do so before one of my ships is destroyed.

'I'm sorry. I – I didn't want to fire. It's not easy, shooting another ship.'

'How strange that a human should say that. Clearly the Space Invaders shot themselves?'

'What do you mean?'

'Were they doing you any harm?'

'Look, you've got the wrong idea,' said Johnny. 'We're not really like that!'

'Excuse me. Things appear differently from where I sit.'

It would have been better if she had shouted, but she didn't. Johnny could have dealt with it if she had been angry. Instead, she just sounded tired and sad. It was the same tone of voice in which she'd spoken about the Space Invaders wreckage.

But he found he was quite angry too.

She couldn't be talking about him.

He picked spiders out of the bath, even if they'd got soapy and didn't have much of a chance. Yet she'd looked at him as if he was Ghengiz the Hun or someone . . . after blowing a ship into *bits*.

'I didn't ask for this, you know! I was just playing a game! I've got problems of my own! I ought to be getting a good night's sleep! That's very important at my age! Why me?'

'Why not?'

'Well, I don't see why I should have to be told how nasty we are! You shoot at us as well!'

'Self-defence.'

'No! Often you shoot first!'

'With humans, we have often found it essential to get our self-defence in as soon as possible.'

'Well, I don't like it! Find someone else!'

He switched off the screen and turned his ship away from the fleet. He half expected the Captain to send some fighters after him, but she did not. She didn't do anything.

Soon the fleet was merely a large collection of yellow dots on the radar screen.

Hah! Well!

They could find their own way home. It wasn't as if they needed him any more. The game was ruined. Who was going to spend hours looking at stars? They'd have to manage without him.

Serve them right. He was doing things for them, and they were only newts.

Occasionally a star went past. You didn't get stars going past in real space. But they had to put them in computer games so that people didn't think they'd got something like Wobbler's *Journey to Alpha Centauri*.

Interesting point. Where was *he* going?

The radar screen went *bing*.

There were ships heading towards him. The dots were green. That meant 'friendly'. But the missiles streaking ahead of them didn't look friendly at all.

Hang on, hang on – what colour was he on their radar?

That was important. Friendly ships were green and enemy ships were yellow. He was a starship. A *human* starship.

But on the other hand, he'd been on the same side as the ScreeWee, so he might show up—

He grabbed the microphone and got as far as 'Um, I—' before the rest of the sentence was spread out, very thin, very small, against the stars.

He woke up.

It was 6:3≡.

His throat felt cold.

He wondered why people made such a fuss about dreams. Dream Boat. Dream River. Dream A Little

57

Dream. But when you got right down to it dreams were often horrible, and they felt *real*. Dreams always started out well and then they went wrong, no matter what you did. You couldn't trust dreams.

And he'd left the alarm set, even though this was Sunday and there was nothing to do on a Sunday. No-one else would be up for hours. It'd be a couple of hours even before Bigmac's brother delivered the paper, or at least delivered the wrong paper. And he was all stiff from sitting at the computer, which wasn't switched on.

Maybe tonight he'd put some stuff on the floor to wake him up.

He went back to bed, and switched the blanket on.

He stared at the ceiling for a while. There was still a model Space Shuttle up there. But one of the two bits of cotton had come away from the drawing pin, so it hung down in a permanent nosedive.

There was something in the bed. He fumbled under the covers and pulled out his camera.

Which meant . . .

Some more fumbling found a rectangle of shiny paper.

He looked at it.

Well, yes. Huh. What'd he expect?

He got up again and turned the computer on, then lay in bed so that he could watch the screen. Still more fake stars drifted past.

Maybe other people were doing this, too. All over the country. All over the world, maybe. Maybe not every computer showed the same piece of game space, so that some people were closer to the fleet than others. Or maybe some people were just persistent, like Wobbler, and wouldn't be beaten.

You saw people like that in J&J Software, sometimes. They'd have a go at whatever new game old Patel had put on the machine, get blown to bits or eaten or whatever, which was what happened to you on your first time, and then you couldn't get rid of them with a crowbar. You learned a bit more, and then you died. That's how games worked. People got worked *up*. They had to beat some game, in the same way that Wobbler would spend weeks trying to beat a program. Some people took it personally when they were blown to bits.

So the ships he'd seen, then, were the ones who wouldn't give up.

But the Captain hadn't been at all grateful to him! It wasn't fair, making him feel like some kind of monster. As if he'd like shooting anyone in cold blood! They'd just totally destroyed another ship. OK, it was attacking them after they had surrendered, but after all it was a only a game . . .

Except, of course, it wasn't a game to the ScreeWee.

And they'd surrendered.

That didn't make them his responsibility, did it? Not the whole time? It had been OK for a little while, but he was getting tired of it.

He padded downstairs in the darkened house and pulled the encyclopedia off its shelf under the video. It had been bought last year from a man at the door, who'd persuaded Johnny's father that it was a good encyclopedia because it had a lot of colour pictures in it. It did have a lot of colour pictures in it. You could grow up knowing what everything looked like, if you didn't mind not knowing much about what it was.

After ten minutes with the index he got as far as

prisoners of war, and eventually to the Geneva Convention. It wasn't something you could illustrate with big coloured pictures so there wasn't much about it, but what there was he read with interest.

It was amazing.

He'd always thought that prisoners were, well, prisoners – you hadn't actually killed them, so they ought to think themselves lucky. But it turned out that you had to give them the same food as your own soldiers, and look after them and generally keep them safe. Even if they'd just bombed a whole city you had to help them out of their crashed plane, give them medicine, and treat them properly.

Johnny stared at the page. It was weird. The people who'd written the encyclopedia – it said inside the cover that they were the Universal Wonder Knowledge Data Printing Inc, of Power Cable, Nebraska – had shoved in all these pictures of parrots and stuff because they were the Natural Wonders of the World, when what was really strange was that human beings had come up with an idea like this. It was like finding a tiny bit of the Middle Ages in the middle of all the missiles and things.

Johnny knew about the Middle Ages because of doing his essay on 'What it felt like to be a peasant in the Middle Ages'. When a knight fell off his horse in battle the other side weren't allowed to open him up with a can opener and torture him, but had to look after him and send him back home after a while, although they were allowed to charge for the service.

On the whole, the ScreeWee were letting him off lightly. According to the Geneva Convention, he ought to be feeding all of them as well.

He put the book back and turned the television on.

That was odd. Someone was complaining that the enemy were putting prisoners of war in buildings that might be bombed, so that they could be bombed by their own side. That was a barbaric thing, said the man. Everyone else in the studio agreed.

So did Johnny, in a way. But he wondered how he would explain something like this to the Captain. Everything made sense a bit at a time. It was just when you tried to think of it all at once that it came out wrong.

There was too much war on television now. He felt it was time to start showing something else.

He went out into the kitchen and made himself some toast, and then tried to scrape the burnt bits off quietly so as not to wake people up. He took the toast and the encyclopedia upstairs and got back into bed.

To pass the time he read some more about Switzerland, which was where Geneva was. Every man in the country had to do army training and keep a gun at home, it said. But Switzerland never fought anyone. Perhaps that made sense somewhere. And what the country used to be known for was designing intricate and ingenious mechanical masterpieces that made a little wooden bird come out and go cuckoo.

After a while he dozed off, and didn't dream at all.

On the screen the fake stars drifted by. After an hour or so a yellow dot appeared in the very centre. After another hour it grew slightly bigger, enough to be seen as a cluster of smaller yellow dots.

Then Johnny's mother, who had come to see where he was, tucked him up and switched it off.

5

If Not You, Who Else?

There was a constant smell of smoke and burnt plastic in the ship now, the Captain noticed. The air conditioners couldn't get rid of it any more. Some of the smoke and burned plastic *was* the air conditioners.

She could feel the eyes of her officers on her. She didn't know how many of them she could count on. She got the feeling that she wasn't very popular.

She looked up into the eyes of the Gunnery Officer.

'You disobeyed my orders,' she repeated.

The Gunnery Officer looked around the control-room with an air of injured innocence.

'But we were being *attacked*,' he said. 'They fired the first shots.'

'I said that we would not fire,' said the Captain, trying to ignore the background murmur of agreement. 'I gave my word to the Chosen One. He was about to fire.'

'But he did not,' said the Gunnery Officer. 'He merely watched.'

'He was about to fire.'

'*About* is too late. The tanker *Kreewhea* is destroyed. Along with half our campaign provisions, I should add . . . *Captain*,' said the Gunnery Officer.

'Nevertheless, an order was directly disobeyed.'

'I cannot believe this! Why can't we *fight*!'

The Captain pointed out of the window. The fleet was passing several more ships of the ancient Space Invader race.

'They fought,' she said. 'Endlessly. And look at them now. And they were only the first. Remember what happened to the Vortiroids? And the Meggazzoids? And the Glaxoticon? Do you want to be like them?'

'Hah. They were primitive. Very low resolution.'

'But there were many of them. And they still died.'

'If we are going to die, I for one would rather die fighting,' said the Gunnery Officer. This time the murmur was a lot louder.

'You would still be dead,' said the Captain.

She thought: There'll be a mutiny if I shoot him or imprison him. I can't fine him because none of us have been paid. I can't confine him to his quarters because . . . she hated to think this . . . we might need him, at the end.

'You are severely reprimanded,' she said.

The Gunnery Officer smirked.

'It will go on your record,' the Captain added.

'Since we will not escape alive—' the Gunnery Officer began.

'That is my responsibility,' said the Captain. 'You are dismissed.'

The Gunnery Officer glared at her.

'When we get home—'

'Oh?' said the Captain. 'Now you think we *will* get home?'

By early evening Johnny's temperature was a hundred and two, and he was suffering from what his mother called Sunday night flu. He was lying in the lovely warm glow that comes from knowing that, whatever happens, there'll be no school tomorrow.

The backs of his eyeballs felt itchy. The insides of his elbows felt hot.

It was what came of spending all his time in front of a computer, he'd been told, instead of in the healthy fresh air. He couldn't quite see this, even in his itchy-eyeball state. Surely the fresh air would have been worse? But in his experience being ill always came of whatever you'd been doing. Parents would probably manage to say it came of taking vitamins and wrapping up nice and warm. He'd probably get an appointment down at the health centre next Friday, since they always liked you to be good and ill by the time you came, so that the doctors could be sure of what you'd got.

He could hear the TV downstairs. He spent twenty minutes wondering whether to get out of bed to switch on his old one, but when he moved there were purple blurs in front of his eyes and a *goioioing* hum in his ears.

He must have managed it, though, because next time he looked it was on, and the colours were much better than usual. There were the newscasters – the black one and the one who looked like his glasses fitted under his skin instead of over the top – and there was the studio, just like normal.

Except that it had the words 'ScreeWee War' in the corner, where there were usually words like 'Budget Shock' or 'Euro Summit'. He couldn't hear what people were saying, but the screen switched to a map of space. It was black. That was the point of space. It was just infinity, huge and black with one dot in it that was everything else.

There was one stubby red arrow in the middle of the

blackness. Several dozen blue ones were heading towards it from the edge of the map. In one corner of the map was a photo of a man talking into a phone.

Hang on, thought Johnny. I'm almost certain there wasn't a BBC reporter with the ScreeWees. They'd have said. Probably there isn't even a CNN one.

He still wasn't getting any sound, but he didn't really need any. It was obvious that humans were closing in on the fleet.

The scene changed. Now it showed a tent some-where, and there was the huge man, standing in front of another copy of the map.

This time the sound came up. He was saying: ' . . . that Johnny? He's no fighter. He's no politician. He goes home when the going gets tough. He runs out on his obligations. But apart from that, hey, he's a real nice kid . . .'

'That's not true!' Johnny shouted.

'It isn't?' said a voice behind him.

He didn't look around immediately. By the sound of it, the voice had come from his chair. And that was much more impossible than the ScreeWee being on television. No-one could sit in that chair. It was full of old T-shirts and books and supper plates and junk. There was a deep sock layer and possibly the Lost Strawberry Yoghurt. No-one could sit down there without special equipment.

The Captain was, though. She seemed quite at home.

He'd only ever seen her face on the screen. Now he could see that she was about two metres long, but quite thin – more like a fat snake with legs than an alligator or a newt. She had two thick, heavy pairs about half-way down, and two pairs of thinner ones at the top, on a set of very complicated shoulders. Most of her was covered in a brown overall; the bits that stuck out – her head, all eight hands or feet, and most of her tail – were a yellow-bronze, and covered in very small scales.

'If you parked out in the road Mrs Cannock opposite will be really mad,' Johnny heard himself say. 'She goes on about my dad leaving his car parked out in the road and it's not even a thousand metres long. So this is a hallucination, isn't it?'

'Of course it is,' said the Captain. 'I'm not sure that real space and game space are connected, except in your head.'

'I saw this film once where spaceships could go anywhere in the universe through wormholes in space,' said Johnny. 'That means I've got a wormhole in my *head*?'

The Captain shrugged, which was a very interesting sight in a being with four arms.

'Watch this,' she said. 'This is very impressive. I expect this will be shown a lot.'

She pointed at the screen.

It showed stars, and a dot in the distance. It got bigger very quickly.

'I think I know that,' said Johnny. 'It's one of your ships. The sort you get on level seven, isn't it?'

'The type, I think, will not matter for long,' said the Captain quietly.

The ship was heading away from the camera. Its rocket exhausts got larger and larger. The camera seemed to be mounted on a . . .

'Missile?' said Johnny weakly.

The screen went blank.

Johnny thought of the dead Space Invader armada, turning over and over in the frosty emptiness between the game stars.

'I don't want to know about it,' said Johnny. 'I don't want you to tell me how many ScreeWee there were on board. I don't want you to tell me what happ—'

'No,' said the Captain, 'I expect you don't.'

'It's not my fault! I can't help what people are like!'

'Of course not.'

The Captain had a nasty way of talking in a reasonable voice.

'We are under attack,' she said. 'Humans are attacking us. Even though we have surrendered.'

'Yes, but you only surrendered to me,' said Johnny. 'I'm just *me*. It's not like surrendering to a government or something. I'm not important.'

'On the contrary,' said the ScreeWee, 'you're the saviour of civilization. You're all that stands between your world and certain oblivion. You are the last hope.'

'But that's not . . . real. That's just what it says at the start of the game!'

'And you did not believe it?'

'Look, it always says something like that!'

'Only you can save mankind?' said the Captain.

'Yes, but it's not really true!'

'If not you, then who else?'

'Look,' said Johnny, 'I *have* saved mankind. In the game, anyway. There aren't any ScreeWee attacking any more. People have to play it for hours to find any.'

The Captain smiled. The shrug had been impressive. But the Captain's mouth was half a metre long.

'You humans are strange,' she said. 'You are warlike. But you make rules! *Rules* of war!'

'Um. I think we don't always obey all those rules,' said Johnny.

Another four-armed shrug.

'Does that matter? Even to have made such rules . . . You think all of life is a game.'

The Captain pulled a small piece of silvery paper out of a pocket of her overall.

'Your attackers have left us too short of food. So, *by your rules*,' she said, 'I must ask for the following: fifteen tonnes of pressed wheat extractions treated with sucrose; ten thousand litres of cold bovine lactation; twenty-five tonnes of the baked wheat extraction containing grilled bovine flesh and trace ingredients, along with chopped and fried tubers and fried and corn-extract-coated rings of vegetables of the allium family; one tonne of crushed mustard seeds mixed with water and permitted additives; three tonnes of exploded corn kernels coated with lactic derivation; ten thousand litres of coloured water containing sucrose and trace elements; fifteen tonnes of prepared and fermented wheat extract in vegetable juice; one thousand tonnes of soured lactic acid flavoured with fruit extract. Daily. Thank you.'

'What?'

'The food of your fighting men,' explained the Captain.

'Doesn't sound like food.'

'You are right,' said the Captain. 'It is disgustingly lacking in fresh vegetables and dangerously high in carbohydrates and saturated fats. However, it appears that this is what you eat.'

'Me? I don't even know what that stuff *is*! What are pressed wheat extractions treated with sucrose?'

'It said "Snappiflakes" on the packet,' said the Captain.

'Soured lactic acid?'

'You had a banana yoghurt.'

Johnny's lips moved as he tried to work this out.

'The grilled bovine flesh and all that stuff?'

'A hamburger and fries with fried onion rings.'

Johnny tried to sit up.

'Are you saying that I've got to go down to the shops and get takeaway Jumboburgers for an entire alien spacefleet?'

'Not exactly.'

'I should think not—'

'My Chief Engineer wants a Bucket of Chicken Lumps.'

'What do ScreeWee usually eat?'

'Normally we eat a kind of waterweed. It contains a perfect balance of vitamins, minerals and trace elements to ensure a healthy growth of scale and crest.'

'Then why—'

'But, as you would put it, it tastes like poo.'

'Oh.'

The Captain stood up. It was a beautiful movement. The ScreeWee body had no *angles* in it, apart from the elbows and knees; she seemed to be able to bend wherever she wanted.

'And now I must return,' she said. 'I hope your attack of minor germs will shortly be over. I could only wish that my attack of human beings was as easily cured.'

'Why aren't you fighting back?' said Johnny. 'I know you can.'

'No. You are wrong. We have surrendered.'

'Yes, but—'

'We will not fire on human ships. Sooner or later, it has to stop. We will run instead. Someone gave us safe conduct.'

The worst bit was that she didn't raise her voice,

or accuse him of anything. She just made statements. Big, horrible statements.

'All right,' said Johnny, in a dull voice, 'but I know it's not real. I've got the flu. You get mild hallucinations when you get the flu. Everyone knows that. I remember I was ill once and all the floppy bunnies on the wallpaper started dancing about. This is like that. You can't really know about this stuff. You're just in my head.'

'What difference does that make?' said the Captain. She stepped out through the wall, and then poked her head back into the room.

'Remember,' she said, 'only you can save mankind.'

'And I said I already—'

'ScreeWee is only the human name for us,' said the Captain. 'Have you ever wondered what the ScreeWee word for ScreeWee is?'

He must have slept, but he didn't dream. He woke up in the middle of the afternoon.

A huge ball of incandescent nuclear fire, heated to millions of degrees, was shining brightly in the sky.

The house was empty. His mother had left him a breakfast tray, which was to say that she'd put together a new Snappiflakes packet, a spoon, a bowl and a note saying 'Milk in Fridge'. She'd also put her office phone number on the bottom of the note. He knew what it was anyway, but sometimes she used the phone number like other people would use an Elastoplast.

He opened the packet and fished around inside. The alien was in a hygienic little paper bag. It was yellow, and in fact did look a bit like the Captain, if you almost shut your eyes.

He wandered aimlessly through the rooms. There

was never anything any good on television in the middle of the day. It was all women talking to one another on sofas. He sneaked a look out into the road, just in case there *were* half-mile-long rocket-exhaust burns. And then he went back upstairs and sat and stared at the silent computer.

OK.

So . . . you switch on. And there's the game. Somehow it felt *worse* thinking about playing it by just sitting in front of it now.

On the other hand, it *was* daytime, so most people would be at school or at least keeping a low profile somewhere. Johnny wasn't quite certain about game time and real time, but maybe the attacks stopped when people had to go to school? But no, there were probably people playing it in America or Australia or somewhere.

Besides, when you died in your sleep you woke up, so what happens now if you die while you're awake?

But the ScreeWee were getting slaughtered out there. Or *in* there. Or in *here*.

The Captain was *stupid* not to fire back.

His hand switched on the computer without his mind really being aware of it.

The game logo appeared. The music started up. The same old message scrolled up the screen. He knew it by heart. Savior of Civilization. Certain Oblivion.

Only You Can Save Mankind.

If Not You, Who Else?

He blinked. The message had scrolled off the top of the screen. He couldn't have imagined that extra last line . . . could he?

And then the same old stars.

He didn't touch the keyboard or the joystick. He

wasn't certain what direction he should be going in. On the whole, straight on seemed best. For hours.

He glanced at the clock. It was just gone four o'clock. People would be home from school now. They'd be watching *Cobbers* and *She'll Be Apples* and *Moonee Ponds*. Bigmac would be watching with his mouth open at his brother's. Wobbler would be watching while trying to rob some other poor computer games writer of his just rewards. Yo-less probably wouldn't be paying much attention, exactly; it'd just be on while he did his homework. Yo-less always did his homework when he got home from school and didn't pay attention to anything else until it had been finished to his satisfaction. But everyone watched *Cobbers*.

Except Johnny, today.

He felt vaguely proud of that. The television was off. He had other things to do.

Somewhere in the last ten minutes he'd made a decision. He wasn't sure exactly what it was, but he'd made it. So he had to see it through. Whatever it was.

He went to the bathroom and had a go with the thermometer. It was an electronic one that his mother had bought from a catalogue, and it also told the time. *Everything* in the catalogue had a digital clock built in. Even the golf umbrella that doubled as a Handy Picnic Table. Even the thing for getting fluff out of socks.

'Away with Not Being Able to Know What the Time is All the Time Blues,' said Johnny vaguely, and stuck the thermometer in his mouth for the required twenty seconds.

His temperature was 16:04°.

No wonder he felt cold.

He went back to bed with the thermometer still in his mouth and looked at the screen again.

Still just stars.

The rest of them would probably be down at the mall now, unless Yo-less was trying for an A+ with his homework. Hanging out. Waiting for another day to end.

He squinted at the thermometer. It read 16:07°.

Still nothing but stars on the screen . . .

6

Chicken Lumps In Space

He woke up. The familiar smell of the starship tickled his nose. He cast his eyes over the control panel. He was getting a bit more familiar with it now.

Right. So he was back in real life again. When he got back to . . . when he got back to . . . He'd have to have a word with the medics about this odd recurring dream that he was a boy in—

No! he thought. I'm me! Not a pilot in a computer game! If I start thinking like that then I'll *really* die! Got to take charge!

Then he noticed the other ships on the screen. He was still a long way from the fleet, of course. But there were three other ships spread out neatly behind him, in convoy. They were bigger and fatter than his and, insofar as it was possible to do this in space, they seemed to wallow rather than fly.

He hit the Communications button. A plump face appeared on the screen.

'Wobbler?'

'Johnny?'

'What are *you* doing in my head?'

The on-screen Wobbler looked around.

'Well, according to this little panel riveted on the control thingy, I'm flying a Class Three Light

Tanker. Wow! Is it normally like this inside your head?'

'I'm not sure,' said Johnny. By the main communication screen was another switch saying 'Conference Facility'. He had a feeling he knew what it did.

Sure enough, when he pressed it Wobbler's face drifted to the top left-hand corner of the screen. Yo-less's face appeared in the opposite corner, with Johnny's own head above it. The other corner stayed blank.

Johnny tapped a button.

'Bigmac?' he said. 'Yo-less?'

Bigmac's face appeared in the blank. He appeared to be wiping his mouth.

'Checking the cargo?' said Johnny sarcastically.

'It's full of hamburgers!' said Bigmac, in a voice like a good monk who's just arrived in heaven and found that all the sins of the flesh are allowed. 'Boxes and boxes of hamburgers! I mean *millions*! With fries. And one Bucket of Chicken Lumps, it says here.'

'It says on this clipboard,' said Yo-less, 'that I'm flying a lot of Prepared Corn and Wheat Products. Shall I go and see what they are?'

'OK,' said Johnny. 'Then that means you're driving the milk tanker, Wobbler.'

'Oh, yes. That's right. Bigmac gets burgers, Wobbler gets boring *milk*,' moaned Wobbler.

Yo-less's face reappeared.

'Back there it's breakfast cereals, mainly,' he said. 'In Giant-Jumbo-Mega-Civilization-Sized boxes.'

'Then Bigmac'd better bring his ship between you and Wobbler,' said Johnny briskly. 'We can't risk a collision.'

'Snap, crackle, *fababababBOOM*!' said Bigmac.

'Will we remember this when we wake up?' said Wobbler.

'How can we?' said Yo-less. '*We're* not dreaming.'

'OK. OK. Um. So will we remember this when *he* wakes up?'

'I don't think so. I think we're only here as projections from his own subconscious mind,' said Yo-less. 'He's just dreaming us.'

'You mean we're not *real*?' said Bigmac.

'I'm not sure if *I'm* real,' said Johnny.

'It *feels* real,' said Wobbler. 'Smells real, too.'

'Tastes real,' said Bigmac.

'Looks real,' said Yo-less. 'But he's only imagining we're here. It's not really us. Just the us that's inside his head.'

Don't ask me, thought Johnny. You were always best at this stuff.

'And I've just worked out, right,' said Yo-less, 'that if we send in the boxtops from every single packet back there we can get six thousand sets of saucepans, OK? And twenty thousand books of football stickers and fifty-seven thousand chances to win a Stylish Five-Door Ford Sierra.'

The four ships lumbered on towards the distant fleet. Johnny's starship could easily outdistance the tankers, so he flew in wide circles around them, watching the radar screen.

There was an occasional zip and sizzle from Wobbler's tanker. He was trying to take its computer apart, just in case there were any design innovations Johnny might remember when he woke up.

Ships appeared on the screen. There was the big dot of the fleet and, around the edges of the screen, the green dots of the game players.

A thought occurred to him.

'Yo-less?'

'Yeah?'

'Have those things got any guns on?'

'Er . . . what do they look like?'

'There's probably a red button on the joystick.'

'Not got one on mine.'

'What about you, Wobbler? Bigmac?'

'Nope.'

'Which one's the joystick?' said Bigmac.

'It's the thing you're steering with.'

'Yeah, wipe the mustard off and have a look,' said Yo-less.

'Nothing on it,' said Bigmac.

Unarmed, thought Johnny. And slow. One hit with a missile and Wobbler is sitting inside the biggest cheese in the universe. What happens to people in my dream?

'Why does it always go *wrong*?

'I'll just go on ahead,' he said, and pressed the Fast button.

There were three players attacking the ScreeWee fleet. It soon became two; Johnny had one in his sights all the way in, curving away through the smoke-ring of the explosion and heading for the next attacker so fast that he was only just behind his own missile.

It was going after the Captain's ship, and the player wasn't paying attention to his radar. Another explosion, already behind Johnny as he looked for the third player.

Johnny realized he wasn't thinking about it. His eyes and hands were doing all the work. He was just watching from inside.

The third player had spotted the tankers. It saw him, turned and actually managed to get some shots away.

Oh, no. Johnny's mind whirred like a machine, judging speed and distance . . .

He felt the ship buck under him, but he held it steady until the crosshairs merged.

Then he pressed his thumb down until a beeping sound told him he hadn't got anything more to fire.

After a while the red mist cleared. He found thoughts slinking back into his mind again. They moved slowly, uncertain of where they were, like people drifting back into a bombed city, picking through rubble, trying to find the old familiar shapes.

There was a metallic taste in his mouth. His elbow ached – he must have banged it on something during the turn.

He thought: No wonder we make rules. The Captain thinks it's strange, but we don't. We know what we'd be like if we didn't have rules.

A light flashed by the communication screen. Someone wanted to talk to him. He flicked a switch.

The face of the Captain appeared.

'*Ah, Johnny. What an efficient technique.*'

'Yes. But I had to—'

'*Of course. And I see you have brought some friends.*'

'You said you needed food.'

'*Even more so now. That last attack was severe.*'

'Aren't you firing at all?'

'*No. We have surrendered, I remind you. Besides, we must not stop. Some of us at least will reach the Border.*'

'Border?' said Johnny. 'I thought you were going to a planet.'

'*We must cross the Border first. Beyond the Border, we are safe. Even you cannot follow us. If we fight, all of us die. If we run, some of us live.*'

'I don't think humans can think like that,' said Johnny. He glanced out of the cockpit. The tankers were getting nearer.

'*You are mammals. Fast. Hot-blooded. We are amphibians. Cold-blooded. Slow. Logical. Some of us will get across. We breed fast. To us, it makes sense. To me, it makes sense.*'

The Captain's image moved to a corner of the screen. Wobbler, Bigmac and Yo-less appeared in the other three quarters.

'That was brilliant shooting,' said Bigmac. 'When I'm in the army—'

'There's a frog on my screen,' said Wobbler.

'It's . . . *she's* the Captain,' said Johnny.

'A woman in charge?' said Yo-less.

'No wonder the aliens always lose,' said Wobbler. 'You should see the side of my mum's car.'

'Um. She can hear you, I think. Don't use sexist language,' said Johnny.

The Captain smiled.

'*I invite your comrades to unload their welcome cargoes,*' she said.

They found out how to do it, eventually. The whole of the middle of the tankers came away as one unit. Small ScreeWee ships, not much more than a seat and a pilot's bubble and a motor, nudged them into the holds of the biggest ships. Without them, the tankers were just a cockpit and engine and a big empty network of girders.

Johnny watched the tank from Yo-less's ship drift gently through the hatch of the Captain's ship.

'Er . . . if when you, you know . . . you're pouring them out of the packet,' he said, 'and you sort of find something plastic falls into your bowl . . . well, it's just a joke. It's not on purpose.'

'Thank you.'

'If you save all the box tops you could probably win a Ford Sierra,' said Yo-less. There was a slight tremble in his voice as he tried to sound like someone who talked to aliens every day. 'You could get your photo in *Competitor's Journal*,' he added.

'That would be very useful. Some of the corridors in this ship are very long.'

'Don't be daft,' said Bigmac. 'He'd – she'd never get the spares.'

'Really? In that case we shall have to go for the six thousand sets of saucepans,' said the Captain.

'How do we get back?' said Wobbler.

'How did you get here?'

Wobbler frowned.

'How *did* we get here?' he said. 'One minute I was . . . was . . . and then here I was. Here we were.'

'Come to that, where did all the milk and burgers come from?' said Bigmac.

'It's all right,' said Yo-less. 'I *told* you. We're not really here anyway. We're just anxiety projections. I read about it in a book.'

'That's a relief, then,' said Wobbler. 'That's worth knowing when you're a billion miles out in space. Anyway . . . so how do we get back?'

'I don't know,' said Johnny. 'I generally do it by dying.'

'Is there some other way?' said Yo-less, after a long, thoughtful pause.

'I don't think there is for me. This is game space. You have to die to get out,' said Johnny. 'I think *you* can probably just fly back. I'm not definitely sure any harm can come to *you*. You're not playing . . . in your heads, I mean.'

'Well—' Wobbler began.

'But I should go soon, if I was you,' said Johnny. 'Before some more players arrive.'

'We'd stay and help,' said Wobbler, 'but there's no guns on these things, you see.'

He sounded worried.

'Yeah. Silly of me not to have dreamed of any,' said Johnny, kindly.

'Yo-less might be right and we're just stuff in your head,' said Wobbler. 'But even people in dreams don't want to die, I expect.'

'Right.'

'You going to be in school tomorrow?'

'Might be.'

'Right. Well, then . . . chow.'

'See you.'

'You hang in there, right, Johnny?' said Yo-less anxiously.

'I'll try to.'

'Yeah, give them aliens hell, my man!' said Bigmac, as the tankers turned.

Johnny could hear them still talking as the three ships accelerated away.

'That was a foe-par, Bigmac. Johnny's on the aliens' side!'

'What? You mean they're on our side?'

'No, they're on their side. And so is he.'

'Whose side are we on, then?'

'We're on his side.'

'Oh. Right. Er. Yo-less?'

'What?'

'So who's on *our* side?'

'Eh? He is, I suppose.'

'So is there *anyone* on the other side?'

The ships became dots on the radar, and then vanished off the edge of the screen.

Where to, Johnny had no idea.

I may have wished them here, or dreamed them, or something. But I mustn't do it again. Maybe they're not really here, but I don't want to see my friends die. I don't want to see *anybody* die.

At least *I'm* on my side.

He scanned the sky. After a while the Captain said: *'You are not leaving?'*

'Not yet.'

'Until you die, you mean.'

Johnny shrugged.

'It's the only way out,' he said. 'Fight until you die. That's how all games go. You just hope you can get a bit further each time.'

There were still no more attackers on the screen. The fleet looked as if it wasn't moving, but it had built up quite a speed. Every second was taking it further from game space. Every second meant that fewer and fewer players would have the patience or determination to go on looking for it.

He helped himself to some of the horrible nourishing soup from its spigot.

'Johnny?'

'Yes?'

'I believe I upset you some time ago by suggesting that humans are bloodthirsty and dangerous'

'Well. Yes. A bit.'

'In that case . . . I would like to say . . . I am grateful.'

'I don't understand.'

'That you are on our side.'

'Yes, but *I'm* not bloodthirsty.'

'Then I think perhaps a little while ago someone else must have been flying your ship?'

'No. It's hard to explain it to you,' said Johnny. First of all, he'd have to be able to explain it to himself.

'Shall I embark upon a less troubling topic of conversation?'

'You don't have to,' said Johnny. 'I mean, you're in charge. You must have things to do.'

'Oh, spaceships fly themselves,' said the Captain. *'They keep going until they hit things. There is little to do. Tend the wounded and so on. I seldom have a chance to talk to humans. So . . . What is sexist?'*

'What?'

'It was a word you used.'

'Oh, *that*. It just means you should treat people as people and, you know . . . not just assume girls can't do stuff. We got a talk about it at school. There's lots of stuff most girls can't do, but you've got to pretend they can, so that more of them will. That's all of it, really.'

'Presumably there's, uh, stuff boys can't do?'

'Oh, *yeah*. But that's just girls' stuff,' said Johnny. 'Anyway, some girls go and become engineers and things, so they can do proper stuff if they want.'

'Transcend the limitations of their sex. Outdo the other sex, even. Yes. It is much the same with us. Some individuals show an awe-inspiring desire to succeed, to make a career in a field not traditionally considered to be appropriate to their gender.'

'You, you mean,' said Johnny.

'I was referring to the Gunnery Officer.'

'But he's a man – I mean, a male.'

'Yes. Traditionally, ScreeWee warriors are female. They are more inclined to fight. Our ancestors used to have to fight to protect their breeding pond. The males do not do battle. But in his case—'

A speck appeared on the radar.

Johnny put down his cup and watched it carefully.

Normally, players headed straight for the fleet. This one didn't. It hovered right on the edge of the screen and stayed there, keeping pace with the ScreeWee ships.

After a while, another dot appeared from the same direction, and kept on coming.

This one at least looked like just another player.

There was a nasty equation at the back of Johnny's mind. It concerned missiles. There were the six missiles per level in *Only You Can Save Mankind*. Once you'd fired them, that was it. So the longer he stayed alive, the less he had to fight with. But all the attacking players would have six missiles each. *He'd* only got four now. When they were gone, it'd just be guns. One missile in the right place would blow him up. Losing was kind of built-in, in the circumstances.

The attacker came on. But Johnny kept finding his gaze creeping to the dot at the edge of the screen. Somehow it had a watchful look, like a shark trailing a leaky airbed.

He switched on the communicator.

'Attacking ship! Attacking ship! Stop now!'

They can't speak, Johnny thought. They're only a player, they're not *in* the game. They can't speak and they can't listen.

He found he'd automatically targeted a missile on the approaching dot. But that couldn't be the only way. Sooner or later you had to talk, even if it was only because you'd run out of things to throw.

The attacker fired a missile. It streaked past Johnny and away, heading on into empty space.

Not real, Johnny thought. You have to think they're not real. Otherwise you can't do it.

'Attacking ship! This is your last chance! Look, I *mean* it!'

He pressed the button. The ship juddered slightly as a missile took off. The attacker was moving fast. So was the missile. They met and became an expanding red cloud. It drifted around Johnny's ship like a smoke ring.

Someone, somewhere, was blinking at their screen and probably swearing. He hoped.

The dot was still on the edge of the screen. It was irritating him, like an itch in a place he couldn't scratch. Because that wasn't how you were supposed to play. You spotted some aliens and you shot at them. That was what the game was supposed to be *about*.

Lurking in the distance and just watching made him uneasy. It looked like the kind of thing people would do if they were . . . well . . .

. . . taking it seriously.

The Captain sat in front of her desk, watching the big screen. She was chewing. Anything was better than waterweed, even – she looked at the packet – even Sugar-Frosted Corn Crackles in cold bovine lactation. Sweet and crunchy, but with odd hard bits in . . .

She inserted a claw into her mouth and poked around among her teeth until she found the offending object.

She pulled it out and looked at it.

It was green, and had four arms. Most of them were holding some sort of weapon.

She wondered again what these things were. The Chief Medical Officer had suggested that they were, in fact, some sort of vermin which invaded food sources. There was a theory among the crew that they were things to do with religion. Offerings to food gods, perhaps?

She put it carefully on one side of her desk. In the right light, she thought, it looked a bit like the Gunnery Officer.

Then she opened the little cage beside the bowl and let her birds out.

There had been things very like alligators among the ScreeWee's distant ancestors, and some habits had been handed down. The Captain opened her mouth fully, which made her lower and upper jaws move apart in a way that would make a human's eyes water.

The birds hopped in, and began to clean her teeth. One of them found a small piece of plastic ray-gun.

The watching ship was moving, still keeping at a great distance, travelling around the fleet in a wide circle. It had watched one more attacker come in; Johnny had got rid of this one with a missile and some shots, although a flashing red light on the panel was suggesting that something, somewhere, wasn't working any more. Probably those secondary pumps again.

He found he was turning the ship all the time to keep the distant dot in front of him.

Johnny?

It was the Captain.

'Yes? Are you watching it?'

'Yes. It is moving between us and the Border. It is in our direct line of flight now.'

'You can't sort of steer around it?'

'There are more than three hundred ships in the fleet. That may be difficult.'

'It seems to be waiting for something. I'll . . . I'll risk going to have a look.'

He let his ship overtake the fleet and run ahead of it, towards the distant dot.

It made no attempt to get out of his way.

It was a starship just like his own. In fact, in a way . . . it *was* his starship. After all, there was only one starship in the entire game, the one You flew to Save Mankind. Everyone was flying the same one . . . in a way.

It hung against the stars, as lifeless as a Space Invader. Johnny moved a bit closer, until he could see the cockpit and even the shape of a head inside. It had a helmet on. Everyone did – it was on the cover of the box. You wore a helmet in a starship. He didn't know why. Maybe the designers thought you were likely to fall off when you went round corners.

He tried the communicator again.

'Hello? Can you hear me?'

There was nothing but the background hiss of the universe.

'I'm pretty sure you can. I've got a feeling about it.'

The tiny blob of the helmet turned towards him. You could no more see through the smoked glass of the helmet than you could through a pair of sunglasses from the outside, but he knew he was being stared at.

'What are you waiting for?' said Johnny. 'Look, I know you can hear me, I don't want to have to—'

The other ship roared into life. It accelerated towards the oncoming fleet on two lances of blue light.

Johnny swore under his breath and kicked his own engines into life. There was no hope of over-taking the attacker. It had a head start, and a starfighter's top speed was a starfighter's top speed.

It was just out of gun range. He raced along behind it.

Ahead, he could see some of the big capital ships of the fleet manoeuvring clumsily out of the way. They spread out slowly, trying to avoid colliding with one another. Seen from the front, it was like watching the petals of a flower opening.

The attacker roared for the middle of the fleet. Then it rolled gently and fired six missiles, one after another. A moment later, two of the small ScreeWee fighters exploded and one of the larger ships spun around as it was hit.

The attacker was already heading for another fighter. Johnny had to admit it – it was beautiful flying. He'd never realized before how badly most players flew. They flew like people who lived on the ground – from right to left and up and down, woodenly. Like someone moving something on a screen, in fact.

But the attacker rolled and twisted like a swallow in flight. And every turn brought another ScreeWee ship under its guns. Even if they had been firing back, it wouldn't have been hit, except by accident. It *pirouetted*.

The Captain's face appeared on the screen.

'*You must stop this!*'

'I'm trying! I'm trying! Don't you think I'm trying!'

The attacker turned. Johnny hadn't thought it was possible for a starship to skid, but this one did. It paused just for a moment as its jets slowed it down, and then accelerated back the way it had come.

Right down his sights.

'Look, *stop!*' he shouted. He had a missile ready. Why even bother to shout? Players *couldn't* hear, they only saw the game on the screen—

'Who are you?'

It was a very clear voice, and very human. The Captain sounded as though she'd learned the language out of a book, but this voice was one that someone had really used since they were about one year old.

'You *can* hear me!'

'Get out of the way, *stupid*!'

The two pilots stared at one another across a distance that was getting smaller very, very fast.

I've heard that before, Johnny thought. That voice. You can hear all the punctuation . . .

They didn't crash – exactly. There was a grinding noise as each starship scraped the length of the other, ripping off fins, ripping open tanks, and then spun drunkenly away.

The control panel in front of Johnny became a mass of red lights. There were cracks racing across the cockpit.

'Idiot!' screamed the radio.

'It's all right,' said Johnny urgently. 'You just wake up—'

His ship exploded.

7

The Dark Tower

It was 16:34° by the thermometer. Time was different in game space.

No matter how often you died, you never got used to it. It wasn't as if you got better with pract—

She'd heard him. Inside the game.

He sat up.

The ScreeWee were inside the game because it was their world. Wobbler and the rest hadn't really been in it; he was pretty sure he'd just dreamed them in because he needed someone to pilot the food tankers.

But he'd heard her in Patel's. That ringing, sharp voice, which made it very clear that its owner thought everyone in the whole world was dim-witted and had to be talked to like a baby or a foreigner.

On the screen, empty space rolled onwards.

He had to find her. Apart from anything else, no-one who flew like that should be allowed anywhere near the ScreeWee.

Wobbler'd probably know who she was.

He found the room moving around him when he stood up. He probably really was ill, he thought. Well, not surprising. What with Trying Times and stupid school and parents trying to be friends and now having to save an entire alien race instead of getting proper sleep, it wasn't surprising.

He made it to the hall and took the phone off its base and brought it back upstairs. He'd just extended the aerial when it rang.

'Um, hello – Blackbury-two-three-nine-nine-eight-zero-who's-that-speaking-please?'

'Is that you? This is me.'

'Oh. Hello, Wobbler.'

'You ill or something?'

'Flu. Look, Wobbler—'

'You seen the papers today?'

'No. Mum and Dad take them to work with them. Wobbler—'

'Thing in the papers about Gobi Software. Hang on . . . says, "NO ENCOUNTERS OF THE TWENTY-FIRST KIND." That's the headline.'

Johnny hesitated.

'What does it say?' he said, very cautiously.

'What does "inundated" mean?'

' 'S'like "overwhelmed",' said Johnny.

'Says that Gobi Software and computer games shops have been . . . inundated with complaints about *Only You Can Save Mankind*. Because they made that offer of five pounds if you shoot all the aliens, and it says people aren't finding any aliens. And Gobi Software are in trouble because of the Trades Descriptions Act. And they keep on using the word *hacker*,' said Wobbler, in the sneering tones of one who knows what a hacker really is and knows that most journalists *don't*. 'And there's a quote from Al Rampa, president of Gobi. He says they're recalling all the games, and if you send back the original discs they'll send you a token for their new game, *Dodge City 1888*. That got four stars in *FAAzzzzAAAP!*.'

Recalling the games . . .

'Yes, but you haven't got the original discs,' said Johnny. 'You hardly ever have any original discs.'

'No, but I know the guy whose brother bought it,' said Wobbler happily. 'So it was just a problem with the game, right? You weren't mental after all.'

'I never said I was mental,' said Johnny.

'No, but . . . well, you know,' said Wobbler. He sounded embarrassed.

'Wobbler?'

'Yes?'

'You know that girl who was in Patel's?'

'Oh, her. What about her?'

'D'you know who she is?'

'She's someone's sister, I think.'

'Whose?'

'Goes to some kind of special school for the terminally clever. She's called Kylie or Krystal or one of those made-up names. What do you want to know for?'

'Oh, nothing. Just because she complained about the game in Patel's, I suppose. Whose sister is she?'

'Some guy called . . . oh . . . Plonker. Yeah. Friend of Bigmac's. You sure you're all right?'

'Yes. Fine. Cheers.'

'Cheers. You going to be in tomorrow?'

' 'Spect so.'

'Cheers.'

'Cheers.'

Bigmac wasn't on the phone. Where Bigmac lived, people hardly even got letters. Even muggers were frightened to go there. People talked about the Joshua N'Clement block in the same way that they probably once talked about the Black Hole of Calcutta or the Spanish Inquisition's reception area.

The tower loomed all alone, black against the sky, like someone's last tooth.

There wasn't much else around the place. There *was* a row of boarded up shops, but you could see where the fire had been. And there was a pub made out of neon lights and red brick; it was called The Jolly Farmer.

The tower had won an award in 1965, just before bits had started falling off. It was always windy. Even on the calmest day, gales whistled icily through the concrete corridors. The place was some kind of wind reservation. If the Joshua N'Clement block had existed a few thousand years ago, people would have come from all over the country to sacrifice to the wind god.

Johnny's father called it Rottweiler Heights. Johnny could hear them barking as he walked up the stairs (the lifts had stopped working in 1966). Everyone in the tower seemed afraid, and mostly they seemed afraid of one another.

Bigmac lived on the fourteenth floor, with his brother and his brother's girlfriend and a pit bull terrier called Clint. Bigmac's brother was reliably believed to be in the job of moving video recorders around in an informal way.

Johnny knocked cautiously, hoping to be loud enough to be heard by the people but quiet enough to be missed by Clint. No such luck. A wall of sound erupted from behind the door.

After a while there was the clink of a chain and the door opened a few centimetres. A suspicious eye appeared at about the height an eye should be, while a metre below there was a certain amount of confused activity as Clint tried to get both eyes and his teeth into the same narrow crack.

'Yeah?'

'Is Bigmac in?'

'Dunno.'

Johnny knew about this. There were only four rooms in the flat. Bigmac's family was huge and lived all over the town, and practically no member of it knew where any other member was until they were quite sure who was asking.

'It's me, Johnny Maxwell. At school.'

Clint was trying to push a fifteen-centimetre-wide head through a five-centimetre-wide hole.

'Oh, yeah.' Johnny felt that he was being carefully surveyed. 'He's down the pub. Yeah.'

'Oh, right,' said Johnny in what he hoped was a normal voice. 'I mean, yeah.'

Bigmac was thirteen. But the landlord of The Jolly Farmer was reputed to serve anyone who didn't actually turn up on a tricycle.

His way home led back past the pub anyway. He agonized a bit about going in. It was all right for Bigmac. Bigmac had been born looking seventeen. But Bigmac turned out to be outside anyway, leaning against the bonnet of a car. He had a couple of friends with him. They watched Johnny intently as he approached, and the one who had been nonchalantly fiddling with the car's door handle stood up and glared.

Johnny tried to swagger a bit.

'Yeah, Johnny,' said Bigmac, in a vague kind of way.

He's different here, Johnny thought. Older and harder.

The other youths relaxed a little. Bigmac knew

Johnny. That made him acceptable, for now.

'Don't often see you up here,' said Bigmac. 'You drinking now or what?'

Johnny got the feeling that asking for a Coke would definitely be bad for his street cred. He decided to ignore the question.

'I'm looking for Plonker,' he said. 'Wobbler said you know him?'

'What d'you want him for?' said Bigmac.

On the wall in school, or down at the mall, Bigmac wouldn't have even asked. But there were different rules here. Like, in school Bigmac tried to hide how good he was at numbers, and up here he had to hide his ability to hold a normal conversation.

Johnny saw a way through.

'Actually I'm looking for his sister,' he said.

One of Bigmac's friends sniggered.

Bigmac took Johnny's arm and led him a little way off.

'What'd you come up here for?' he said. 'You could've asked me tomorrow.'

'It's . . . important.'

'Bigmac! You coming or what?'

Bigmac glanced over his shoulder.

'Can't,' he said. 'Got to sort out something else.'

One of the kids said something to the other one, and they both laughed. Then they got into the car. After a little while it started up, bumped up on to the pavement and off again, and then accelerated into the night. They heard the tyres screech as it turned the corner on the wrong side of the road.

Bigmac relaxed. Suddenly he was a lot less tough, and a bit shorter, and more like the amiable not-quite-thicko Johnny had always known.

'Didn't you want to go with them?' said Johnny.

'You're a right nerd, aren't you,' said Bigmac, in a friendly enough voice.

'Wobbler says you have to say dweeb now, not nerd,' said Johnny.

'I usually say dickhead. Come on, let's go,' said Bigmac. ''Cos there'll probably be some unhappy people around here pretty soon. 'S'their own fault for leaving a car here.'

'What?'

'Dweeb. You don't know nothing about real life, you.'

'It's just games,' said Johnny, half to himself. 'All different sorts. Bigmac?'

Somewhere away in the distance a car horn wailed, and was suddenly cut off. Bigmac stopped walking. The breeze blew his T-shirt against him, so that 'Terminator' was superimposed on a chest that looked like a toast rack.

'What?' he said.

'Look, have you ever wondered what's real and what isn't?'

'Bloody stupid thing to wonder,' said Bigmac.

'Why?'

'*Real's* real. Everything else isn't.'

'What about . . . well, dreams?'

'Nah. They're not real.'

'They've got to be *something*. Otherwise you couldn't have them, right?' said Johnny desperately.

'Yeah, but that's not the same as *really* real.'

'Are people on television real?'

''Course!'

'Why're we treating them as a game, then?'

'You mean . . . on the News—'

'Yes!'

'That's different. You can't have people going around doing what they like.'

'But *we*—'

'Anyway, space games aren't real,' said Bigmac. He kept looking down the dark street.

Johnny relaxed a little.

'Are you real?'

'Dunno. Feel real. It's all crap anyway.'

'What is?'

'Everything. So who cares? Come on, I'm going back home.'

They strolled past what had been, in 1965, an environmental green space and was now a square of dog-poisoned earth where the shopping trolleys went to die.

'Plonker's a bit of a maniac,' said Bigmac. 'Bit of a wild man. Bit of a loony. Lives in a big posh house, though.'

'Where?'

'Oh, in Tyne Avenue or Crescent or somewhere,' said Bigmac.

A blue light lit his face for a moment as a police car flashed past the end of the road, its siren dee-dahing into the distance.

Bigmac froze.

'What's his real name?' said Johnny.

'Eh? Yeah. Garry, I think.'

Bigmac was staring at the end of the road. The blue light was still visible. It had stopped about half a mile away; they could see it reflected off an advertising hoarding.

'Just Garry?' said Johnny.

Bigmac's face was wet in the light of the street lamps.

Johnny realized that he was sweating.

'Might be Dunn,' said Bigmac. He shifted uneasily from one foot to the other.

Another siren echoed around the night. An ambulance went past on the main road, ghostly under its flashing light.

'Look, Bigmac—'

'Bugger off!'

Bigmac turned and ran, his Doc Marten's crashing on the pavement. Johnny watched him go. He thought of all the things he should have said. He wasn't stupid. Everyone knew what happened to cars around the dark tower. What could he say now?

And his body thought: You don't say anything. You *do* something. It started running all by itself after his friend, taking his brain with it.

Despite a bedroom full of weight-training equipment that would have been of considerable interest if the police had ever bothered much about a recent theft down at the Sports Centre, Bigmac wasn't in much of a condition. He had been *born* out of condition. Johnny caught him up on the bend.

'I told you . . . to . . . buggeroff! Nothing . . . todo . . . withyou!' said Bigmac, as they headed towards the distant lights.

'They crashed it, didn't they.'

'Nozzer's a good driver!'

'Yeah? Good at going fast?'

There was a crowd standing around at the traffic lights further down the road. As they ran, another ambulance overtook them and rocked to a halt. The crowd parted. Johnny caught a glimpse of – well, not a car, but maybe what a car would look like after trying to be in the same place as a liquid-cement truck. He knew it was a cement truck, because one had climbed up the pavement and lay on its side. Its load was fast becoming the biggest brick in the world.

In the distance there was the scream of a fire engine, getting nearer.

He grabbed Bigmac's arm, pulling him around.

'I don't think you want to go any closer,' he said.

Bigmac shook himself free, just as the police managed to lever the crumpled door open.

Bigmac stared.

Then he turned, tottered over to a low garden wall by the roadside, and was sick.

When Johnny reached him his whole body was shaking, with cold and terror.

'Bugger you, I could have been in that, you—'

Bigmac was sick again, all down the front of Arnold Schwarzenegger. Johnny took his coat off and put it over the other boy's shivering shoulders.

'—they kept goin' on at me, I told them, I said—'

'Yeah. Yeah, that's right,' said Johnny, looking around. 'Look, you just sit here . . . there's a phone— You just sit there, all right? You just—'

'*Don't go away!*'

'What? Oh. Yes. Right. Come on then—'

Click!

'Hello, this—'

'Yo-less? It's Johnny.'

'Yes?'

'Your mum in the hospital tonight?'

'No, she's on days this week. Why?'

'Can you get her to bring her car down to Witheridge Road?'

'What's up? You sound as if you've been—'

'Look, shut up! Get her to do it, right? Please! It's Bigmac!'

'What's up with him?'

'Yo-less! This is *important*! This is *really important*!'

'You know how she goes on when I—'

'Yo-less!'

'Oh, all right. Hey, is that a siren?'

'We're in a phone box. You'd better get her to bring a blanket or something. And hurry up, it's dead smelly in here.'

'That was a siren, wasn't it?'

'Yes.'

He put the phone down.

Bigmac wasn't being sick any more. He hadn't got anything to be sick with. He was just leaning against the door, shaking.

'She'll be along right away,' said Johnny, as cheerfully as he could manage. 'She's a ward sister. She knows all about this stuff.'

Outside, one of the ambulances drove away. Firemen were all over the wreck. Some of them were getting equipment off the engine.

Bigmac stared at the scene.

'They're probably fine,' lied Johnny. 'It's amazing how people can—'

'Johnny?'

'What?'

'No-one's fine who looked like that,' said Bigmac, in a flat voice. 'There was blood all over.'

'Well—'

'My brother'll kill me when he finds out. He said if I have the cops round again he'll throw me out of the window. He'll kill me if he finds out.'

'He won't, then. You didn't do anything. We were just hanging out and you felt ill. That's all.'

'He'll kill me!'

'What for? No-one knows anything except me, and I don't know *anything*. I promise.'

It was gone eight when Johnny got home. He left his coat in the shed until he could sneak it in and sponge it off, and said he'd been round at Yo-less's, which was true, and was a pretty good way of avoiding questions, because his parents approved of Yo-less on racial grounds. To object to him being round at Yo-less's would be like objecting to Yo-less. Yo-less was dead handy.

Anyway, it wasn't as if anyone had cooked any dinner. Mrs Yo-less had made him a hot chocolate when he was there, but he hadn't accepted a meal, because that suggested you didn't have them all that often at home and you didn't do that. She'd put Bigmac to bed. Bigmac with his skinhead haircut.

He microwaved himself something called a Pour-On Genuine Creole Lasagne, which said it served four portions. It did if you were dwarfs.

The phone went as he was carrying it upstairs. It was Wobbler.

'Yo-less just rang me.'

'Right.'

'Why didn't you get them to put Bigmac in an ambulance?'

'Who with?'

There was a moment of silence from Wobbler as he worked this out. Then he said, 'Yuk.'

'Right.'

'Anyway, people'd ask questions. Bigmac's been in enough trouble as it is, what with his brother and one thing and another.'

'Right.'

'Wow!'

'Got to go now, Wobbler. Got to eat my dinner before it congeals.'

He put the phone down on the tray, and looked at it. There was something else he was going to do. What was it? Something, anyway.

The lasagne looked real. It looked as though someone had already eaten it once.

The Captain looked up.

Most of her officers were standing in front of her. Except for the Gunnery Officer, who was looking smug, they all wore rather embarrassed expressions.

'Yes?' said the Captain.

To her surprise, it wasn't the Gunnery Officer who spoke. It was the Navigation Officer, a small and inoffensive ScreeWee who suffered for prematurely shedding scales.

'Um,' she said.

'Yes?' said the Captain again.

'Um. We – that is, all of us—' said the Navigation Officer, looking as if she wished she was somewhere else, '—we feel that, uh, the present course is, uh, an unwise one. With respect,' she added.

'In what way?' said the Captain. She could see the Gunnery Officer grinning behind the little ScreeWee. No-one could grin like a ScreeWee – their mouths were built for it.

'We, uh – that is, all of us – we are still being attacked. And that last attack was a terrible one.'

'The Chosen One stopped it, at the cost of his own life,' said the Captain.

'Um. He will return,' said the Navigation Officer. 'Um. Twenty of our people will not.'

The Captain wasn't really looking at her. She was staring at the Gunnery Officer, whose grin was now wide enough to hold a set of billiard balls and probably the cue too.

He's been talking to them, she told herself. Everyone's on edge, no-one can think straight, and he's talking to them. I should have had him shot. They wouldn't have liked it, but I could probably have shouted them down.

'So what is it you are suggesting?' she said.

'Um. We – that is, all of us,' said the little ScreeWee, with an imploring glance at the Gunnery Officer, 'we feel we should turn and—'

'Fight?' said the Captain. 'Make a last stand?'

'Um. Yes. That's right.'

'And that's the feeling of all of you?'

The officers nodded, one after another.

'Um. Sorry, ma'am,' said the Navigation Officer.

'The others stood and fought,' said the Captain. 'The . . . Space Invaders. And the others. We've all seen the wrecks. All they knew was how to attack. They stood and fought, and fought and died.'

'We are dying too, um,' said the Navigation Officer.

'I know. I am sorry,' said the Captain. 'But many are living. And every minute takes us further from danger. We are so near the Border! If we stop . . . you know what will happen. Game space will move. The Border will retreat. The humans will find us. And then they will—'

'Die,' said the Gunnery Officer. 'And we shall win.

Those others were stupid. We are not. We can win. We shall give the humans the mother of all battles.'

'Ah, yes,' said the Captain. 'Mother and grandmother of battles. Battles that breed more battles.'

'And this is your leader speaking,' sneered the Gunnery Officer. 'The leader of the fleet. It is pathetic. Cowardly.'

'When we are home—' the Captain began.

'Home? This is our home! We have no other! All this talk of the Border, and a planet of our own . . . Have any of us seen it? No! It's a legend. Wishful thinking. A dream. We lie to ourselves. We make up stories. The Chosen One. The Hero with a Thousand Extra Lives! It's all dreams! We live and breed and die on our ships. That is our destiny. There is no choice!'

8

Peace Talks, Peace Shouts

Johnny awoke in the starship.

Normally he was some way from the fleet, but this time it was around him. There were ScreeWee ships on every side.

They were flying the wrong way.

Immediately, a face appeared on the screen. Except for a few differences on the crest, and a slight orange tint to the scales, it might have been the Captain.

'*Calling the human ship.*'

'Who are you?'

'*I am the new Captain. These are my instructions—*'

'What happened to the old Captain?'

'*She is under arrest. These are my instructions—*'

'Arrest? What for? What did she do?'

'*She did nothing. Listen to me. You have sixty seconds to get beyond range of our guns. For honour. After that, you will be fired upon with extreme force.*'

'Hang on—'

'*The count has started.*'

'But—'

'*End of communication. Die, human.*'

The screen went blank.

Johnny stared at it.

It hadn't been a friendly face. The voice had sounded

as though it had learned Human out of a book, just like the real Captain. But in this case it had been a nasty book. It also sounded as though it belonged to someone who would count to sixty like this: 'One, two, three, four, five, seven, eighteen, thirty-five, forty-nine, fifty-eight, fifty-nine, sixty – firing, ready or not—'

His ship jerked forward, ramming him back in his seat. That was one good thing about game space – you could do the kind of turns and manouevres that, in real space, would leave the human body looking like thin pink lino across the cabin wall . . .

The fleet slid past, dwindling to a collection of dots behind him. A couple of laser beams crackled past, but some way away; it looked as though they were trying to frighten him off rather than kill him.

The ScreeWee had turned around. They were heading back deeper into game space. Why? They'd show up on people's screens soon! There were always some players who'd go looking. Any day now some kid'd switch on his machine and there'd be wall-to-wall ScreeWee, heading straight for him. They weren't safe even now. Yes – there were always some people who'd go looking . . .

And there was a green dot ahead of him. He recognized the way it moved, like a dog creeping around the edge of a sheep field.

He headed towards it.

Now he could remember. You thought better in game space, too. It was as if he was more *him* in game space. Krystal or Kylie or one of those made-up names, Wobbler had said. And Bigmac said the other name was Dunn . . .

He twirled the knob of the communicator panel.

'Krystal?' he tried. 'Kylie? Kathryn? Whatever?'

There was just the hiss of the stars, and then: 'It's Kirsty, *actually*.'

'Don't fire!' said Johnny, quickly.

'Who *are* you?'

'Don't fire, first. Promise? I hate dying. It makes it hard to think.'

The other ship had stopped being a dot now. If she was going to fire, he was as good as dead – if dead was good.

'All right,' she said, slowly. 'No firing. Peace talk. Now tell me who you are.'

'I'm a player, like you,' said Johnny.

'No you're not. None of the other players talk to me. Anyway, you're on *their* side. I've been watching you.'

'Not . . . exactly on *their* side,' said Johnny.

'Well, you're not on *my* side,' said Kirsty. 'No-one is.'

'Did they try to surrender to you too? I heard you say in Patel's shop that they'd sent you a message.'

There was another silence filled with the whispers of the universe, and then a cautious voice: 'You're not the fat one who looks as though he could do with a bra, are you?'

'No. Listen—' Johnny tapped his controls hurriedly.

'The black one who looks like an accountant?'

'No. *Look*—'

'Oh, no . . . not the *skinny* one with the big boots and the pointy head . . . ?'

'No, I'm the one who kind of hangs around and no-one notices much,' said Johnny desperately.

'Who? I didn't see anyone.'

'Right! *That was me!*'

'They surrendered to *you*?'

'Yes!' Number three missile went ping as it locked on to her ship. Now for number four—

'But you're a nerd!'

Ping!

'I think it's dweeb now. Anyway, I'm more than a dweeb.'

Ping!

'Why?'

'I'm a dweeb with five missiles targeted on you.'

'You said you weren't going to fire!'

'I haven't yet.'

'You said this was a peace talk!'

'*You* did. Anyway, it is. It's just that I'm . . . kind of shouting.'

If he concentrated, he thought he could hear music in the background when she spoke.

'You've *really* got missiles targeted on me?'

'Yes.'

'I'm amazed you thought of it.'

'So am I. Look, I don't want to shoot *anyone*. But I need help. The fleet's turned round. They fired at me!'

'That's their *job*, dweeb. They fire at us, we fire at them. Why did they stop? It's no fun if they don't fire back.'

'They surrendered.'

'They can't surrender. It's a game.'

'Well, they did. Sometimes you change the game. I don't know, Kirsty!'

'Listen, I hate that name!'

'I've got to call you something,' said Johnny. 'What do you call yourself?'

'If you tell anyone else I'll kill you—'

'I thought you were planning to do that anyway.'

'I don't mean just kill you, I mean *really* kill you.'

'All right. What's your game name?'

'Sigourney – *you're laughing!*'

'I'm not! I'm not! It was a sneeze! Honest! No, it's a . . . good name. Very . . . appropriate . . .'

'It's just dreaming, anyway. I'm dreaming this. You're dreaming this.'

'So what? Doesn't make things unimportant.'

There was some more silence with the scratchy suggestion of music in the background, and then: 'Ah-*ha!* While we've been talking, Mr Clever, *I've* targeted missiles on *you!*'

Johnny shrugged, even though there was no way she could see that.

'Doesn't matter. I thought you would, anyway. So we kill each other. Then we'll have to go through all this again. It's stupid. Don't you want to find out what happens next?'

More scratchy music.

'I can hear scratchy music,' said Johnny.

'It's my Walkman.'

'Clever. I wish I'd thought of that. I tried dreaming my camera, but the pictures weren't any good. What're you listening to?'

'C Inlay 4 Details – "Please Keep This Copy For Your Records".'

There was another scratchy pause.

Then, as if she'd been thinking deeply, she said: 'Look, we can't be in the same dream. That can't happen.'

'We could find out. Where'd you live?'

This time the pause went on for a long time. The ScreeWee fleet appeared on the radar.

'We'd better move,' said Johnny. 'They've started

firing. Something's happened to the Captain. She's the one that wanted peace in the first place. Look, I know you live in Tyne Avenue or Crescent or somewhere—'

'How come we live so close?'

'Dunno. Bad luck, I suppose. Look, they're going to be in range soon—'

'No problem. Then we shoot them.'

'We'll be killed. Anyway—'

'So what? Dying's easy.'

'I know. It's living that's the problem,' said Johnny, meaning it. 'You don't sound like someone who takes the easy way.'

C Inlay 4 Details played on in the distance.

'So what do you have in mind?'

Johnny hesitated. He hadn't thought that far. The new Captain didn't seem to want to talk.

'Dunno. I just don't want any ScreeWee to get killed.'

'Why not?'

Because when they die, they die for real.

'I just don't, OK?'

Several fighters had left the fleet and were heading purposefully towards them.

'I'm going to try and talk one more time,' he decided. 'Someone must be listening.'

'Nerdy idea.'

'I'm not much good at the other kind.'

Johnny turned his ship and hit the Go-faster button. A few shots whiffled harmlessly past him and did a lot of damage to empty space.

And then he was heading at maximum speed towards the fleet.

Music came over the intercom.

'Idiot! Dodge and dive! No wonder you get shot a lot!'

He wiggled the joystick. Something clipped one of the starship's wings and exploded behind him.

'*And* you've got the fighters after you! Huh! You can't even save yourself!'

Johnny didn't take his eyes off the fleet, which was bouncing around the sky as he flung his ship about in an effort to avoid being shot at.

'You might try to be some help!' he shouted.

There was a boom behind him.

'I am.'

'You're shooting them?'

'You're very hard to please, *actually*.'

The Captain tried the door of her cabin again. It was still locked. And there was almost certainly a guard in the corridor outside. ScreeWee tended to obey orders, even if they didn't like them. The Gunnery Officer was very unusual.

That, she thought bitterly, is what comes of promoting a male. They're unreliable thinkers.

She looked around the cabin. She didn't want to be in it. She wanted to be outside it. But she was in it. She needed a new idea.

Humans seemed much better at ideas. They always seemed to be on the verge of being totally insane, but it seemed to work for them. The inside of their heads would be an interesting place to visit, but she wouldn't want to live there.

How do you think like a human? Go into madness first, probably, and then out the other side . . .

'Listen! *Listen!* If you keep going this way, you'll all

be killed! You're going back into game space! People like me will find you! You'll all be killed! That's how it goes!'

And then he died.

It was 6.3 ≡ . He was lying on his bed with his clothes on, but he still felt cold.

Bits and pieces of his . . . his previous life trickled through his mind.

Sigourney!

Well, Yo-less would say that explained anything. And now it looked as if he'd be spending every night watching the ScreeWee get killed.

It was bad enough fighting off people in ones and twos. But they were just the ones who were weird or lonely or bored enough to go looking. Wobbler said thousands of copies of the game had been sold. Even if most people took them back to the shops, there'd always be someone playing. Once the ScreeWee turned up again, the news would get around . . .

And then, one day, long after no-one played the game any more, there'd be these broken ships, turning over and over in the blank-screen darkness of game space.

And he couldn't stop it. Kir — Sigourney was right. That's what they were *there* for.

It was Tuesday, too. It was Maths for most of the morning. And then English. He'd better write a poem at lunchtime. You could generally get away with a poem.

He got his jacket out of the shed and sponged it off as best he could, and then propped it up by the heater. Then he investigated the fridge.

His father had been doing the shopping again. You

could always tell. There were generally expensive things in jars, and odd foreign vegetables. This time there was Yoghurt Vindaloo and more celery. No-one in the house liked celery much. It always ended up going brown. And his father never bought bread and potatoes. He seemed to think that stuff like that just *grew* in kitchens, like mushrooms (although he always bought mushrooms, if they were the special expensive dried kind that looked like bits of mouldy bark and were picked by wizened old Frenchmen).

There was a carton of milk which thumped when he shook it.

Johnny found a cup in the ghastly cavern of the dishwasher and rinsed it under the tap. At least there wasn't much that could go wrong with black coffee.

He quite enjoyed the time by himself in the mornings. The day was too early to have started going really wrong.

The war was still on television. It was getting on his nerves. It was worrying him. You'd really think everyone would have had enough by now.

Bigmac was in school. He'd stayed the night at Yoless's. Mrs Yo-less had washed out his clothes, even the T-shirt with 'Blackbury Skins' on the back. It was a lot cleaner than it had ever been.

He could feel Wobbler and Yo-less looking at him with interest. So were one or two other people.

Later on, when they were in the middle of the rush which meant that every pupil in the school had to walk all the way across the campus to be somewhere else, Yo-less said: 'Bigmac said you pulled him out of the wreck. Did you?'

'What? He wasn't even—' Johnny paused.

It was amazing. He'd never thought so fast before. He thought of Bigmac's room, with its Weapons of the World posters and plastic model guns and weight-training stuff he couldn't lift. Bigmac had been thrown out of the school role-playing games club for getting too excited. Bigmac, who spent all his time trying hard to be a big thicko; Bigmac, who could work out maths problems just by looking at them. Bigmac, who played the game of being . . . well, big tough Bigmac.

Johnny looked around. Bigmac was watching him. It was amazing, given that Bigmac's ancestors were a sort of monkey, how much his expression looked like the one he'd first seen on the face of the Captain, whose ancestors were a kind of alligator. It said: Help me.

'Can't really remember,' he said.

'Only my mum rang the hospital and they said there were only two boys and they were—'

'It was dark,' said Johnny.

'Yes, but if you'd *really*—'

'It's just best if everyone shuts up about it, all right?' said Johnny, nodding meaningfully at Bigmac.

'She said you did everything right, anyway,' said Yo-less. 'And she said you aren't being properly looked after.'

'Yo-*less*.'

'She said you ought to come round our house to eat sometimes—'

'Thanks,' said Johnny. 'I'm a bit busy these days—'

'Doing what?' said Yo-less.

Johnny fumbled in his pocket.

'What does this look like to you?' he said.

Yo-less took it gravely.

'It's a photograph,' he said. 'Just looks like a TV screen with dots on.'

'Yes,' sighed Johnny. 'It does, doesn't it.'

He took it back and shoved it deep into his pocket. 'Yo-less?'

'What?'

'If someone was . . . you know . . . going a bit weird in the head—'

'Mental, he means,' said Wobbler, behind him.

'Just a bit *over-strained*,' said Johnny. 'I mean . . . would they know? Themselves?'

'Well, everyone thinks they're a bit mad,' said Yo-less. 'It's part of being normal.'

'Oh, I don't think I'm mad,' said Johnny.

'You don't?'

'Well—'

'Ah-*aha!*' said Wobbler.

'I mean – the whole world seems kind of weird right now. You watch the telly, don't you? How can you be the good guys if you're dropping clever bombs right down people's chimneys? And blowing people up just because they're being bossed around by a loony?'

'Shouldn't let 'emselves be bossed around, then,' said Bigmac. Johnny looked at him. Bigmac deflated a bit. 'It's their own fault. They don't *have* to. That's what my brother says, anyway,' he mumbled.

'Is it?' said Johnny.

Bigmac shrugged.

'Oh, well, *yes*,' said Wobbler. 'How? It's hard enough to get rid of prime ministers and at least they don't have people taken out and shot. Not any more, anyway.'

'My brother's *stupid*,' said Bigmac, so quietly under

his breath that Johnny wondered if anyone else even heard it.

'There was a man on the box saying that the bomb-aimers were so good because they all grew up playing computer games,' said Wobbler.

'See?' said Johnny. 'That's what I mean. Games look real. Real things look like games. And . . . and . . . it all kind of runs together in my head.'

'Ah,' said Yo-less, knowingly. 'That's not mental. That's shamanism. I read a book about it.'

'What's shamanism?'

'Shamans used to be these kind of people who lived partly in a dream world and partly in the real world,' said Wobbler. 'Like medicine men and druids and guys like that. They used to be very important. They used to guide people.'

'Guide?' said Johnny. 'Where to?'

'Not sure. Anyway, my mother says they were creations of Satan.'

'Yes, but your mother says that about practically everything,' said Wobbler.

'This is true,' said Yo-less gravely. 'It's her hobby.'

'She said role-playing games were creations of Satan,' said Wobbler.

'True.'

'Dead clever of him,' said Wobbler. 'I mean, sitting down there in Hell, working out all the combat tables and everything. I bet he used to really *swear* every time the dice caught fire . . .'

Shamanism, thought Johnny. Yes. I could be a shaman. A guide. That's better than being mental, at any rate.

It was Maths *again*. As far as Johnny was concerned,

the future would be a better place if it didn't contain $3y + x^2$. He had problems enough without people giving him pages of them.

He was trying to put off the idea of ringing someone up.

And then there was Social Education. Normally you could ignore Social Education, which tended to be about anything anyone had on their minds at the time or, failing that, Aids. Really the day ended with Maths. SE was just there to keep you off the streets for another three-quarters of an hour.

He *could* try ringing up. You just needed the phone book and a bit of thought . . .

Johnny stared at the ceiling. The teacher was going on about the war. That was all there was to talk about these days. He listened with half an ear. No-one liked the bombing. One of the girls was nearly in tears about it . . .

Supposing *she* was really there? Or supposing *she* said she'd never heard of him?

Bigmac was arguing. That was unusual.

And then someone said, 'Do you think it's easy? Do you think the pilots *really* just sit there like . . . like a game? Do you think they laugh? Really laugh? Not just laugh because they're still alive, but laugh because it's . . . it's fun? When they're being shot at for a living, every day? When any minute they might get blown up too? Do you think they don't wonder what it's all about? Do you think they *like* it? But we always turn it into something that's not exactly real. We turn it into games and it's not games. We really have to find out what's *real*!'

They were all looking at him.

'Anyway, that's what I think,' said Johnny.

9

On Earth, No-one Can Hear You
Say 'Um'

Click!

'Yes?'

'Um.'

'Hello?'

'Um. Is Sig – is Kirsty there?'

'Who's that?'

'I'm a friend. Um. I don't think she knows my name.'

'You're a friend and she doesn't know your name?'

'Please!'

'Oh, hang on.'

Johnny stared at his bedroom wall. Eventually a suspicious voice said, 'Yes? Who's that?'

'You're Sigourney. You like C Inlay 4 Details. You fly really well. You—'

'You're *him*!'

Johnny breathed a sigh of relief. Real!

Going through the phone book had been harder than flying the starship. Nearly harder than dying.

'I wasn't sure you really existed,' he said.

'I wasn't sure *you* existed,' she said.

'I've got to talk to you. I mean face to face.'

'How do I know you're not some sort of maniac?'

'Do I *sound* like some sort of maniac?'

'Yes!'

'All right, but apart from that?'

There was silence for a moment. Then she said, reluctantly: 'All right. You can come round here.'

'What? To your house?'

'It's safer than in public, idiot.'

Not for me, Johnny thought.

'OK,' he said.

'I mean, you might be one of those funny people.'

'What, clowns?'

And then she said, very cautiously: 'It's really you?'

'*Really* I'm not sure about. But me, yes.'

'You got blown up.'

'Yes, I know. I was there, remember.'

'I don't die often in the game. It took me ages even to find the aliens.'

Huh, thought Johnny.

'It doesn't get any better with practice,' he said, darkly.

Tyne Crescent turned out to be a pretty straight road with trees in it, and the houses were big and had double garages and a timber effect on them to fool people into believing that Henry VIII had built them.

Kirsty's mother opened the door for him. She was grinning like the Captain, although the Captain had the excuse that she was related to crocodiles. Johnny felt he had the wrong clothes on, or the wrong face.

He was shown into a large room. It was mainly white. Expensive bookshelves lined one wall. Most of the floor was bare pine, but varnished and polished to show that they could have afforded carpets if they'd wanted them. There was a harp standing by a chair in one corner, and music scattered around it on the floor.

Johnny picked up a sheet. It was headed 'Royal College, Grade V'.

'Well?'

She was standing behind him. The sheet slipped out of his fingers.

'And don't say "um",' she said, sitting down. 'You say "um" a lot. Aren't you ever sure about things?'

'U— No. Hello?'

'Sit down. My mother's making us some tea. And then staying out of the way. You'll probably notice that. You can actually *hear* her staying out of the way. She thinks I ought to have more friends.'

She had red hair, and the skinny look that went with it. It was as if someone had grabbed the frizzy ponytail on the back of her head and pulled it tightly.

'The game,' said Johnny vaguely.

'Yes? What?'

'I'm really glad you're in it too. Yo-less said it was all in my head because of Trying Times. He said it was just me projecting my problems.'

'*I* haven't got any problems,' snapped Kirsty. 'I get on extremely well with people, *actually*. There's probably some simple psychic reason that you're too stupid to work out.'

'You sounded more concerned on the phone,' said Johnny.

'But now I've had time to think about it. Anyway, what's it to me what happens to some dots in a machine?'

'Didn't you see the Space Invaders?' said Johnny.

'Yes, but they *were* stupid. That's what happens. Charles Darwin knew about that. I am a winning kind of person. And what I want to know is, what were you doing in *my* dream?'

'I'm not sure it's a dream,' said Johnny. 'I'm not sure *what* it is. Not exactly a dream and not exactly real. Something in between. I don't know. Maybe something happens in your head. Maybe you're in there because – because, well, I don't know why, but there's got to be a reason,' he ended lamely.

'Why're *you* there, then?'

'I want to save the ScreeWee.'

'Why?'

'Because . . . I've got a responsibility. But the Captain's been . . . I don't know, locked up or something. There's been some kind of mutiny. It's the Gunnery Officer. He's behind it. But if I – if we could get her out, she could probably turn the fleet around again. I thought you might be able to think of some way of getting her out,' Johnny finished lamely. 'We haven't got a lot of game time.'

'She?' said Kirsty.

'She started all this. She relied on me,' said Johnny.

'You said "she",' said Kirsty.

Johnny stood up.

'I thought you might be able to help,' he said wearily, 'but who cares what happens to some dots that aren't even real. So I'll just—'

'You keep saying "she",' said Kirsty. 'You mean the Captain's a woman?'

'A female,' said Johnny. 'Yes.'

'But you called the Gunnery Officer a "he",' said Kirsty.

'That's right.'

Kirsty stood up.

'That's typical. That's absolutely typical of modern society. He probably resents a wo – a female being better than him. I get that *all the time*.'

121

'Um,' said Johnny. He hadn't meant to say 'um'. He meant to say: 'Actually, all the ScreeWee *except* the Gunnery Officer are females.' But another part of his brain had thought faster and shut down his mouth before he could say it, diverting the words into oblivion and shoving good old 'um' in their place.

'There was an article in a magazine,' said Kirsty. 'This whole bunch of directors of a company ganged up on this woman and sacked her just because she'd become the boss. It was just like me and the Chess Club.'

It probably wouldn't be a good idea to tell her. There was a glint in her eye. No, it probably wouldn't be a good idea to be honest. Truthfulness would have to do instead. After all, he hadn't actually *lied*.

'It's a matter of principle,' said Kirsty. 'You should have said so right at the start.' She stood up. 'Come on.'

'Where are we going?' said Johnny.

'To my room,' said Kirsty. 'Don't worry. My parents are very liberal.'

There were film posters all over the walls, and where there weren't film posters there were shelves with silver cups on. There was a framed certificate for the Regional Winner of the Small-Bore Rifle Confederation's National Championships, and another one for chess. And another one for athletics. There were a lot of medals, mostly gold, and one or two silver. Kirsty won things.

If there was a medal for a tidy bedroom, she would have won that too. You could see the floor all the way to the walls.

She had an electrical pencil sharpener.

And a computer. The screen was showing the familiar message: NEW GAME (Y/N)?

'Do you know I have an IQ of one hundred and sixty-five?' she said, sitting down in front of the screen.

'Is that good?'

'Yes! And I only started playing this *wretched* game because my brother bought it and said I wouldn't be any good at it. These things are *moronic*.'

There was a notebook by the keyboard.

'Each level,' explained Kirsty. 'I made notes about how the ships flew. And kept score, of course.'

'You were taking it seriously,' said Johnny. 'Very seriously.'

'Of *course* I take it seriously. It's a *game*. You've got to *win* them, otherwise what's the point? Now . . . can we get on to the ScreeWee flagship?'

'Um—'

'Think!'

'Can we get into a ScreeWee battleship?'

Kirsty almost growled. 'I asked *you*. Sit down and *think*!'

Johnny sat down.

'I don't think we can,' he said. 'I'm always in a starship. I think things have to look like they do on the screen.'

'Hmm. Makes some sort of sense, I suppose.' Kirsty stuck a pencil in the sharpener, which whirred for a while. 'And we don't know what it looks like inside.'

Johnny stared at the wall. Among the items pinned over the bed was a card for winning the Under-7 Long Jump. She wins everything, he thought. Wow. She actually assumes she's going to win. Someone who always thinks they're going to win . . .

He stared up at the movie posters. There was one he'd seen many times before. The famous one. The slavering alien monster. You'd think she'd have something like a C Inlay 4 Details photo over her bed but no, there was this thing . . .

'Don't tell me,' he said, 'you want to get inside the ship and run along the corridors shooting ScreeWee? You do, don't you?'

'Tactically—' she began.

'You can't. The Captain wouldn't want that. Not killing ScreeWee.'

Kirsty waved her hands in the air irritably.

'That's *stupid*,' she said. 'How do you expect to win without killing the enemy?'

'I'm supposed to save them. Anyway, they're not exactly the enemy. I can't go around killing them.'

Kirsty looked thoughtful.

'Do you know,' she said, 'there was an African tribe once whose nearest word for "enemy" was "a friend we haven't met yet"?'

Johnny smiled. 'Right,' he said. 'That's how—'

'But they were all killed and eaten in eighteen hundred and two,' said Kirsty. 'Except for those who were sold as slaves. The last one died in Mississippi in eighteen sixty-four, and he was *very upset*.'

'You just made that up,' said Johnny.

'No. I won a prize for History.'

'I expect you did,' said Johnny. 'But I'm not killing anyone.'

'Then you *can't* win.'

'I don't want to win. I just don't want them to lose.'

'You really *are* a dweeb, aren't you? How can anyone go through life expecting to lose all the time?'

'Well, I've got to, haven't I? The world is full of people like you, for a start.'

Johnny realized he was getting angry again. He

didn't often get angry. He just got quiet, or miserable. Anger was unusual. But when it came, it overflowed.

'They tried to talk to you, and you didn't even listen! You were the only other one that got that involved! You were so mad to win you slipped into game space! And you'd have been so much better at saving them than me! And you didn't even listen! But I listened and I've spent a week trying to Save Mankind in my sleep! It's always people like me that have to do stuff like that! It's always the people who aren't clever and who don't win things that have to get killed all the time! And you just hung around and watched! It's just like on the television! The winners have fun! Winner types never lose, they just come second! It's all the other people who lose! And now you're only thinking of helping the Captain because you think she's like you! Well, I don't bloody well care any more, Miss Clever! I've done my best! And I'm going to go on doing it! And they'll all come back into game space and it'll be just like the Space Invaders all over again! And I'll be there every night!'

Her mouth was open.

There was a knock on the door and almost immediately, mothers being what they are, Kirsty's mother pushed it open. She brought in a wide grin and a tray.

'I'm sure you'd both like some tea,' she said. 'And—'

'*Yes*, mother,' said Kirsty, and rolled her eyes.

'—there's some macaroons. Have you found out your friend's name now?'

'John Maxwell,' said Johnny.

'And what do your friends call you?' said Kirsty's mother sweetly.

'Sometimes they call me Rubber,' said Johnny.

'Do they? Whatever for?'

'*Mother*, we were *talking*,' said Kirsty.

'*Cobbers* is on in a minute,' said Kirsty's mother. 'I, er, shall watch it on the set in the kitchen, shall I?'

'Goodbye,' said Kirsty, meaningfully.

'Um, yes,' said her mother, and went out.

'She dithers a lot,' said Kirsty. 'Fancy getting married when you're twenty! A complete lack of ambition.'

She stared at Johnny for a while. He was keeping quiet. He'd been amazed to hear his own thoughts.

Kirsty coughed. She looked a little uncertain, for the first time since Johnny had met her.

'Well,' she said. 'Uh. OK. And . . . we won't be able to fight all the players when they get back to game space.'

'No. There's not enough missiles.'

'Could we dream a few more?'

'No. I thought of that. You get the ship you play with. I mean, we *know* it's only got six missiles. I've tried dreaming more and it doesn't work.'

'Hmm. Interesting problem. *Sorry*,' she added quickly, when she saw his expression.

Johnny stared at the movie posters. Sigourney! Games everywhere. Bigmac was a tough guy in his head, and *this* one kept sharp pencils and had to win everything and in her head shot aliens. Everyone had these pictures of themselves in their head, except him . . .

He blinked.

And now his head ached. There was a buzzing in his ears.

Kirsty's face drifted towards him.

'Are you all right?'

The headache was really bad now.

'You're ill. And you look all thin. When did you last eat?'

'I dunno. Had something last night, I think.'

'Last night? What about breakfast and lunch?'

'Oh, well . . . you know . . . I kept thinking about . . .'

'You'd better drink that tea and eat that macaroon. Phew. When did you last have a bath?'

'It's kind of . . .'

'Good grief—'

'Listen! Listen!' It was important to tell her. He didn't feel well at all.

'Yes?'

'We dream our way in,' he said.

'What are you talking about? You're swaying!'

'We go on to their ship!'

'But we agreed we don't know what it looks like inside!'

'OK! Good! So we decide what it *does* look like inside, right?'

She tapped her pad irritably.

'So what does it look like?'

'I don't know! The inside of a spaceship! Corridors and cabins and stuff like that. Nuts and bolts and panels and sliding doors. Scotsmen saying the engines canna tak' it anymoore. Bright blue lights!'

'Hmm. That's what you think is inside spaceships, is it?'

Kirsty glared at him. She generally glared. It was her normal expression.

'When we go to sleep . . . I mean, when I go to sleep . . . I'll try and wake up inside the ship,' he said.

'How?'

'I don't know! By concentrating, I suppose.'

She leaned forward. For the first time since he'd met her, she looked concerned.

'You don't look capable of thinking straight,' she said.

'I'll be all right.'

Johnny stood up.

10

In Space, No-one Is Listening *Anyway*

And woke up.

He was lying down on something hard. There was some sort of mesh just in front of his eyes. He stared at it for a while.

There was also a faint vibration in the floor, and a distant background rumbling.

He was obviously back in game space, but he certainly wasn't in a starship . . .

The mesh moved.

The Captain's face appeared over the edge of the mesh, upside down.

'Johnny?'

'Where am I?'

'You appear to be under my bed.'

He rolled sideways.

'I'm on your ship?'

'Oh, yes.'

'Right! Hah! I knew I could do it . . .'

He stood up, and looked around the cabin. It wasn't very interesting. Apart from the bed, which was under something that looked like a sun-ray lamp, there was only a desk and something that was probably a chair if you had four back legs and a thick tail.

On the desk were half a dozen plastic aliens. There

was also a cage with a couple of long-beaked birds in it. They sat side by side on their perch and watched Johnny with almost intelligent eyes.

Right. Sigourney was right. He *did* think better in game space. All the decisions seemed so much clearer.

OK. So he was on board. He'd rather hoped to be *outside* the cabin the Captain was locked in, but this was a start.

He stared at the wall. There was a grille.

'What's that?' he said, pointing.

'It is where the air comes in.'

Johnny pulled at the grille. There was no very obvious way of removing it. If it *could* be removed, the hole behind it was easily big enough for the Captain. Air ducts. Well, what did he expect?

'We've got to get this off,' he said. 'Before something dreadful happens.'

'We are imprisoned,' said the Captain. 'What more can happen that is dreadful?'

'Have you ever heard the name . . . Sigourney?' said Johnny cautiously.

'No. But it sounds a lovely name,' said the Captain. 'Who is this Sigourney?'

'Well, if she can dream her way here as well, then there's going to be *trouble*. You should see the pictures she's got on her walls.'

'What of?'

'Um. Aliens,' said Johnny.

'She takes a very close interest in alien races?' said the Captain happily.

'Um. Yes.' The mere thought of her arrival made him pull urgently at the grille. 'Um. There's something on the inside . . . and I can't quite get my hand through . . .'

The Captain watched him with interest.

'Something like wingnuts,' grunted Johnny.

'This is very instructive,' said the Captain, peering over his shoulder.

'I can't get a grip!'

'You wish to turn them?'

'Yes!'

The Captain waddled over to the table and opened the bird cage. Both of the birds hopped out on to her hand. The Captain said a few words in ScreeWee; the birds fluttered past Johnny's head, squeezed through the mesh, and disappeared. After a second or two he heard the squeak-squeak of nuts being undone.

'What were they?' he said.

'Chee,' said the Captain. 'Mouth birds. You understand?' She opened her mouth, revealing several rows of yellow teeth. 'For hygiene?'

'Living toothbrushes?'

'We have always had them. They are . . . traditional. Very intelligent. Bred for it, you know. Clever things. They understand several words of ScreeWee.'

The squeaking went on. There was a clonk, and a nut rolled through the mesh.

The panel fell into the room.

Johnny looked at the hole.

'O-*kay*,' he said uncertainly. 'You don't know where it goes, do you?'

'No. There are ventilation shafts all over the ship. Will you lead the way?'

'Um—'

'I would be happy for you to lead the way,' said the Captain.

Johnny stood on the bed and crawled into the hole. It went a little way and then opened on to a bigger shaft.

'All over the ship?' he said.

'Yes.'

Johnny paused for a moment. He'd never liked narrow dark spaces.

'Oh. Right,' he said.

Kirsty's mother put down the phone.

'There's no-one answering,' she said.

'I think he said his father works late and his mother sometimes works in the evening,' said Kirsty. 'Anyway, the doctor said he's basically all right, didn't she? He's just run down, she said. What was the stuff she gave him?'

'She said it'd make him sleep. He's not getting enough sleep. Twelve-year-old boys need a lot of sleep.'

'I know this one does,' said Kirsty.

'And *you* said he's not eating properly. Where did you meet him, anyway?'

'Um,' Kirsty began, and then smiled to herself. 'Out and about.'

Kirsty's mother looked worried.

'Are you sure he's all there?'

'He's all there,' said Kirsty, climbing the stairs. 'I'm not sure that he's all *here*, but he's certainly all there.'

She opened the door of the spare room and looked in. Johnny was fast asleep in a pair of her brother's pyjamas. He looked very young. It's amazing how young twelve is, when you're thirteen.

Then she went to her own bedroom, got ready for bed, and slid between the sheets.

It was pretty early. It had been a busy evening.

He was a loser. You could tell. He *dressed* like a loser. A ditherer. Someone who said 'um' a lot, and went through life trying not to be noticed.

She'd never done that. She'd always gone through life as if there was a big red arrow above the planet, indicating precisely where she was.

On the other hand, he *tried* so hard . . .

She'd bet he'd cried when ET died.

She pushed herself up on one elbow and stared at the movie posters.

Trying wasn't the point.

You had to win. What good was anything if you didn't win?

'Stuck? You're an *alien*,' said Johnny. 'Aliens don't get stuck in air ducts. It's practically a well-known fact.'

He backed into a side tunnel, and turned around.

'I am sorry. It occurs to me that possibly I am the wrong type of alien,' said the Captain. 'I can go backwards, but I am forwardly disadvantaged.'

'OK. Back up to that second junction we passed,' said Johnny. 'We're lost, anyway.'

'No,' said the Captain, 'I know where we are. It says here this is junction ⊨ ⊋ ⊖.'

'Do you know where that is?'

'No.'

'I saw a film where there was an alien crawling around inside a spaceship's air ducts and it could come out wherever it liked,' said Johnny reproachfully.

'Doubtless it had a map,' said the Captain.

Johnny crawled around a corner and found . . .

. . . another grille.

There didn't seem to be any activity on the other side of it. He unscrewed the nuts and let it fall on to the floor.

There was a corridor. He dropped into it, then turned and helped the Captain through. ScreeWee might have descended from crocodiles, but crocodiles preferred sandbanks. They weren't very good at crawling through narrow spaces.

Her skin felt cold and dry, like silk.

There were no other ScreeWee around.

'They're probably at battle stations,' said Johnny.

'We're *always* at battle stations,' said the Captain bitterly, brushing dust off her scales. 'This is corridor ⚸. Now we must get to the bridge, yes?'

'Won't they just lock you up again?' said Johnny.

'I think not. Disobedience to properly constituted authority does not come easily to us. The Gunnery Officer is very . . . persuasive. But once they see that I am free again, they will give in. At least,' the Captain added, 'most of them will. The Gunnery Officer may prove difficult. He dreams of grandeur.'

She waddled a little way along the bare corridor, keeping close to the wall. Johnny trailed behind her.

'Dreams are always tricky,' he said.

'Yes.'

'But they'll wake up when the players start shooting again, won't they? They'll soon see what he is leading them into?'

'We have a proverb,' said the Captain. '*SkeejeeshejweeJEEyee*. It means . . .' she thought for a moment, 'when you are riding a *jee*, a six-legged domesticated beast of burden capable of simple instruction but also traditionally foul-tempered, it is easier to stay on rather than dismount; equally, better to trust yourself to a *jee* than risk attack from the sure-footed *JEEyee*, which will easily outrun a ScreeWee on foot. Of course, it is a little snappier in our language.'

They'd reached a corner. The Captain peered around it, and then jerked her head back.

'There is a guard outside the door of my cabin,' she said. 'She is armed.'

'Can you talk to her?'

'She is under orders. I fear that I will only be allowed to say "Aaargh!",' said the Captain. 'But feel free to make the attempt. I have no other options.'

Oh, well – you only die a few hundred times, thought Johnny. He stepped out into the corridor.

The guard turned to look at him, and half raised a melted-looking thing that nevertheless very clearly said 'gun'. But she looked at him in puzzlement.

She's never seen a human before! he thought.

He spread his arms wide in what he hoped was an innocent-looking way, and smiled.

Which just goes to show that you shouldn't take things for granted because, as the Captain told him later, when a ScreeWee is about to fight she does two things. She spreads her front pairs of arms wide (to grip and throttle) and exposes her teeth (ready to bite).

The guard raised the gun.

Then there was a thunderous knocking on the other side of the cabin door.

The guard made a simple mistake. She *should* have ignored the knocking, loud and desperate though it was, and concentrated on Johnny. But she tried to keep the gun pointing in his general direction while she pressed a panel by the door. After all, it was only the Captain in there, wasn't it? And the Captain was still the Captain, even if she was locked up. She could keep an eye on both of them . . .

The door opened a little way. A foot came out, swinging upwards, and caught the guard under the snout. There was a click as all its teeth met. Its eyes crossed.

Someone shouted: 'Haiii!'

The guard swayed backwards. Kirsty came through the door airborne and started hacking at the guard's arms with her hands. It dropped the gun. She picked it up in one movement. The guard opened its mouth to bite, spread its arms to grip and throttle, and then went cross-eyed because the gun barrel was suddenly thrust between its teeth.

'Don't . . . swallow . . .' said Kirsty, very deliberately.

There was a sudden, very heavy silence. The guard stayed very still.

'This is a friend of mine,' said Johnny.

'Oh, yes,' said the Captain. 'Sigourney. One of your warriors. Is she a friend of mine?'

'At the moment,' said Sigourney, without moving her head. She had tied one of the strips of webbing from the Captain's bed around her forehead. She was breathing heavily. There was a wild glint in her eye. Johnny suddenly felt very sorry for the guard.

'You know, I'm *glad* she's a friend of mine,' said the Captain.

'Ee ee ogg ee?' said the guard. Its arms were trembling. The ScreeWee didn't sweat, but this one would probably have liked to.

'We'd better tie her up and put her in the cabin,' said Johnny.

'Ees!' said the guard.

'I could just fire,' said Sigourney wistfully.

'No!' said Johnny and the Captain together.

'Eep!' said the guard.

'Oh, all right.' Sigourney relaxed. The guard sagged.

'Sorry to be late,' said Sigourney. 'Had a bit of trouble getting to sleep.'

The Captain said something to the guard in ScreeWee. It nodded in a strangely human way and trooped obediently into the cabin, where it squatted down just as obediently and let them tie its hands and feet with more bits of bed.

'You've got a black belt in karate too, I expect,' said Johnny.

'Only purple,' she said. 'But I haven't been doing it long,' she added quickly. 'Huh! Is that the only kind of knot you can tie?'

'I went to karate once, with Bigmac,' said Johnny, trying to ignore that.

'What happened?'

'I got my foot caught in my trousers.'

'And *you* are the Chosen One? Huh! They could have chosen *me*.'

'They tried. But *I* was the one who listened,' said Johnny quietly.

Sigourney picked up the gun and cradled it in her arms.

'Well, I'm here now,' she said, 'And ready to kick some butt.'

'Some but what?' said Johnny wearily. He really hated the phrase. It was a game saying. It tried to fool you into believing that real bullets weren't going to go through real people.

Sigourney sniffed.

'Nerd.'

They went back into the corridor.

'By the way,' said Johnny, 'what happened to me?'

'You just collapsed. Right there on the floor. We've got a doctor living next door. Mum went and got her. Unusually bright of her, really. She said you were just

137

tired out and looked as though you hadn't been eating properly.'

'This is true,' said the Captain. 'Did I not say? Too much sugar and carbohydrate, not enough fresh vitamins. You should get out more.'

'Yeah, right,' said Johnny.

There was something different about the corridor. Before, it had been grey metal, only interesting if you really liked looking at nuts and bolts. But now it was darker, with more curves; the walls glistened, and dripped menace. Dripped something, anyway.

The Captain looked different, too. She hadn't changed, exactly – it was just that her teeth and claws were somehow more obvious. A few minutes ago, she had been an intelligent person who just happened to be an eight-legged crocodile; now she was an eight-legged crocodile who just happened to be intelligent.

Game space was changing now two people were sharing one dream.

'Hold on, there's—' he began.

'Don't let's hang around,' said Sigourney.

'But you're—' Johnny began.

Dreaming it wrong, he finished to himself.

This really *is* nuts, he told himself as he trailed after them. At home Kirsty went around being Miss Brains. In here it was all: Make my shorts! Eat my day!

The Captain waddled at high speed along the corridors. Now steam was dribbling from somewhere, making the floor misty and wet.

There wasn't that much in the ScreeWee ships. Perhaps they ought to have sat down and worked out the inside of one in a bit more detail before they'd dreamed, he thought. They could have added more cabins and big screens and interesting things like that;

as it was, all there seemed to be were these snaking corridors that were unpleasantly like caves.

Bigger caves, though. They'd got wider. Mysterious passages led off in various directions.

Sigourney crept along with her back against the wall, spinning around rapidly every time they passed another passage. She stiffened.

'There's another one coming!' she hissed. 'It's pushing something! Get back!'

She elbowed them into the wall. Johnny could hear the scrape-scrape of claws on the floor, and something rattling.

'When it gets closer I'll get it. I'll leap out—'

Johnny poked his head around the corner.

'Kirsty?'

She took no notice.

'Sigourney?' he tried.

'Yes?'

'I know you're going to leap out,' said Johnny, 'but don't pull the trigger, right?'

'It's an *alien*!'

'So it's an alien. You don't have to shoot them all.'

The rattling got closer. There was also a faint squeaking.

Sigourney gripped the gun excitedly, and leapt out.

'OK, *you* – oh . . . um . . .'

It was a very small ScreeWee. Most of its scales were grey. Its crest was nearly worn away. Its tail just dragged behind it. When it opened its mouth, there were three teeth left and they were huddling together at the back.

It blinked owlishly at them over the top of the trolley it had been pushing. Apart from anything else, Kirsty had been aiming the gun well above its head.

There was one of those awkward pauses.

'Around this time,' said the Captain behind them, 'the crew on the bridge have a snack brought to them.'

Johnny leaned forward, nodded at the little old alien, and lifted the lid of the tray that was on the trolley. There were a few bowls of something green and bubbling. He gently lowered the lid again.

'I think you were going to shoot the tea lady,' he said.

'How was I to know?' Kirsty demanded. 'It could have been anything! This is an alien spaceship! You're not supposed to get *tea ladies*!'

The Captain said something in ScreeWee to the old alien, who shuffled around slowly and went off back down the corridor. One wheel of the trolley kept squeaking.

Kirsty was furious.

'This isn't going right!' she hissed.

'Come on,' said Johnny. 'Let's go to the bridge and get it over with.'

'I didn't *know* it was a tea lady! That's *your* dreaming!'

'Yes, all right.'

'She had no right to be there!'

'I suppose even aliens get a bit thirsty in the afternoons.'

'That's not what I meant! They're supposed to be *alien*! That means slavering and claws! It doesn't mean sending out for . . . for a coffee and a jam doughnut!'

'Things are just like they are,' said Johnny, shrugging.

She turned on him.

'Why do you just *accept* everything? Why don't you ever try to *change* things?'

'They're generally bad enough already,' he said.

She leapt ahead and peered around the next corner.

'Guards!' she said. 'And these have got *guns*!'

Johnny looked around the corner. There were two ScreeWee standing in front of a round door. They were, indeed, armed.

'Satisfied?' she snapped. 'No hint of Danish pastries anywhere? Right? Now can I actually shoot something?'

'No! I keep telling you! You have to give them a chance to surrender.'

'You always make it difficult!'

She raised the gun and stepped out.

So did the Captain. *She* hissed a word in ScreeWee. The guards looked from her to Kirsty, who was squinting along her gun barrel. One of them hissed something.

'She says the Gunnery Officer has instructed them to shoot anyone who approaches the door,' said the Captain.

'I'll fire if they move,' said Kirsty. 'I mean it!'

The Captain spoke in ScreeWee again. The guards stared at Johnny. They lowered their guns.

Suspicion rose inside him.

'What did you just tell them?' he said.

'I just told them who you were,' said the Captain.

'You said I was the Chosen One?'

One of the guards was trying to kneel. That looked very strange in a creature with four legs.

Kirsty rolled her eyes.

'It's better than being shot at,' said the Captain. 'I've been shot at a lot. I know what I am talking about.'

'Tell her to get up,' said Johnny. 'What do we do now? Who's on the bridge?'

'Most of the officers,' said the Captain. 'The guard says there have been – arguments. Gunfire.'

'That's more like it!' said Kirsty.

They looked at the door.

'OK,' said Johnny. 'Let's go . . .'

The Captain motioned one of the guards aside and touched a plate by the door.

11

Humans!

Johnny saw it all in one long, long second.

Firstly, the bridge was *big*. It seemed to be the size of a football pitch. And at one end there was a screen, which looked almost as big. He felt like an ant standing in front of a TV set.

The screen was covered with green dots.

Players. Heading for the fleet.

There were hundreds of them.

Right in front of the screen was a horseshoe-shaped bank of controls, with a dozen seats ranged in front of it.

It's here, he thought. When I was sitting in my room playing, they were in here in this great shadowy room, steering their ship, firing back . . .

Only one seat was occupied now. Its occupant was already standing up, half turning, reaching for something . . .

'Go ahead,' said Kirsty. 'Make my stardate.'

The Gunnery Officer froze, glaring at them.

'Too late,' he said. 'You're too late!' He waved a claw towards the screen. 'I've taken us back to where we belong. There is no time to turn us round again. You *must* fight now.'

He focused on Johnny. 'What's *that*?' he said.

'The Chosen One,' said the Captain, starting to walk forward. The others followed her.

'But we *must* fight,' said the Gunnery Officer. 'For honour. The honour of the ScreeWee! That's what we are *for*!'

Johnny's foot touched something. He looked down. Now that his eyes had become accustomed to the gloom, he could see that he'd almost tripped over a ScreeWee. It was dead. Nothing with a hole like that in it could have been alive.

Kirsty was looking down, too. Johnny could see other shapes on the floor in the shadows.

'He's been killing Sc – people,' he whispered.

Shoot them in space, shoot them on a screen, and there was just an explosion and five points on the score total. When they'd been shot from a few metres away, then there was simply a reminder that someone who had been alive was now, very definitely, not alive any more. And would never be again.

He looked up at the Gunnery Officer. ScreeWee were cold-blooded and a long way from being human, but this one had a look about it – about *him* that suggested a mind running off into madness.

There was a silvery sheen on his scales. Johnny found himself wondering if the ScreeWee changed colour, like chameleons. The Captain had always looked more golden when she was acting normally, and became almost yellow when she was worried . . .

She was the colour of lemons now.

She hissed something. The guards looked at her in surprise, but turned and filed obediently out of the bridge. Then she turned to the Gunnery Officer.

'You killed all of them?' she said, softly.

'They tried to stop me! It is a matter of honour!'

'Yes, yes. I can see that,' said the Captain, in a level voice. She was shifting position slightly now, moving away from the humans.

'A ScreeWee dies fighting or not at all!' shouted the Gunnery Officer.

The Captain's scales had faded to the colour of old paper.

'Yes, I understand, I understand,' she said. 'And the humans understand too, *don't you*.'

The Gunnery Officer turned his head. The Captain spread her arms, opened her mouth and leapt. The male must have sensed her; he turned, claws whirring through the air.

Johnny reached out and caught Kirsty's gun as she raised it.

'No! You might hit her!'

'Why'd she do that? I could easily have shot him! So could the guards! Why just jump at him like that?'

The fighters were a whirling ball of claws and tails.

'It's personal. I think she hates him too much,' he said. 'But look at the screen!'

There were more green dots. Red figures that might have meant something to a ScreeWee were scrolling up on one side too fast for a human to read.

He looked down at the controls.

'They're getting closer! We've got to do something.'

Kirsty stared at the controls too. The seats were made to fit a ScreeWee. So were the controls themselves.

'Well, do *you* know what $\odot \quad \nabla \quad \leftrightharpoons \quad \overline{\mp} \quad \geq$ means?' she said. 'Fast? Slow? Fire? The cigarette lighter?'

The fighters had broken apart and were circling each other, hissing. The green and red light from the screen threw unpleasant shadows.

Neither ScreeWee was paying the humans the least attention. They couldn't afford to. ScreeWee walked like ducks and looked like a cartoon of a crocodile, but they fought like cats – it was mainly watching and snarling with short, terrible blurs of attack and defence.

A light started to flash on the panel and an alarm rang. It rang in ScreeWee, but it was still pretty urgent even in Human.

The Captain spun around. The Gunnery Officer jumped backwards, hit the ground running, and sped towards the door. He was through it in a blur.

'He can't go anywhere,' said the Captain, staggering across to the controls. 'I . . . can deal with him later . . .'

'You've got some nasty scratches,' said Kirsty. ScreeWee blood was blue. 'I know some first aid . . .'

'A lot, I expect,' said Johnny.

'But not for ScreeWee, I imagine,' said the Captain. Her chest was heaving. One of her legs seemed to be at the wrong angle. Blue patches covered her tail.

'You could have just shot him,' said Kirsty. 'It was stupid to fight like that.'

'Honour!' snarled the Captain. She tripped a switch with a claw and hissed some instructions in ScreeWee. 'But he was right. Sadly, I know this now. There is no changing ScreeWee nature. Our destiny is to fight and die. I have been foolish to think otherwise.'

She blinked.

'Take off your shirt,' Kirsty demanded.

'What?' said Johnny.

'Your shirt! Your shirt! Look at her! She's losing blood! She needs bandaging!'

Johnny obeyed, reluctantly.

'You've got a vest on underneath? Only grandads wear a vest. Yuk. Don't you ever wash your clothes?'

He did, sometimes. And occasionally his mother had a burst of being a mother and everything in the house got washed. But usually he used the wash-basket laundry, which consisted of going through the basket until he found something that didn't seem all that bad.

'But she said you wouldn't know anything about ScreeWee medicine,' he said.

'So what? Even if it's blue, blood's still blood. You should try to keep it inside.'

Kirsty helped the Captain to a chair. The alien was swaying a bit, and her scales had gone white, speckled with blue.

'Is there anything I can do?' said Johnny.

Kirsty glanced at him. 'I don't know,' she said. 'Is there *anything* you can do?'

She turned back to the Captain.

We'll all die, Johnny thought. They're all out there waiting. And here's me at the controls of the main alien ship. We can't turn round now. And I can't even read what it says on the controls!

I've done it all wrong. It was all simple, and now it's all complicated.

You think about doing things in dreams, but we're always wrong about dreams. When people talk about dreams they mean *day*dreams. *That's* where you're Superman or whatever. That's where you win everything. In dreams everything is weird. I'm in a dream now. Or something like a dream. And when I wake up, all the ScreeWee will be back in game space and they'll be shot at again, just like the Space Invaders.

Hang on . . .

Hang on . . .

He stared at the meaningless controls again.

On one of them the symbols $\triangleq \; \odot \; \mathcal{Y} \; \leftrightarrows \; \neg$

147

rearranged themselves to form 'Main Engines'.

This is *my* world, too. It's in my head.

He looked up at the big screen.

All of them. They're all there, waiting. In bedrooms and lounges around the world. In between watching *Cobbers* and doing their homework.

All waiting with their finger on the Fire button, and each one thinking that they're the only one . . .

All there, in front of *me* . . .

'I wasn't expecting to do this,' said Kirsty, behind him. 'I wasn't expecting to be bandaging aliens. Put a claw on this knot, will you? What's your pulse level?'

'I don't think we have them,' said the Captain.

The ship *thumped*.

The distant background rumble of the engines was suddenly a roar.

The seats had bits sticking up where humans didn't expect bits to stick up. Johnny was sitting cross-legged on one, both hands on the controls, face multi-coloured in the light of the screen.

Kirsty tapped him on the shoulder. 'What *are* you doing?'

'Flying,' said Johnny, without turning his head.

'He said it's too late to turn round.'

'I'm not turning round.'

'You don't know how to fly one of these!'

'I'm not flying one of these. I'm flying the whole fleet.'

'You can't understand the controls!'

Green and red light made patterns on his face as he turned to her.

'You know, everyone tells me things. All the time,' he said. 'Well, I'm not listening now. I can read the controls. Why not? They're in my head. Now sit down. I shall need you to do some things. And stop talking to me as if I'm stupid.'

She sat down, almost hypnotized by his tone of voice.

'But *how*—'

'There's a control that lets this ship steer all the others as well. It's used on long voyages.' He moved a lever. 'And I'm flying them as fast as I can. I don't think they can go any faster. All the dials have gone into the ＼ $\hbar$ ⊗ – that's ScreeWee for red.'

'But you're heading straight for the players!'

'I've got to. There isn't time to turn round . . .'

Wobbler had a pin-up over his bed. It was a close-up photograph of the Intel 80586–75 microprocessor, taken through a microscope; it looked like a street map of a very complicated modern city. His grandfather complained that it was unhealthy and why didn't he have a double page spread from *Giggles and Garters* instead, but Wobbler had a vision: one day, if he could master GCSE maths and reliably pick up a soldering iron by the end that wasn't hot, he was going to be a Big Man in computers. A Number One programmer, with his hair in a ponytail at the back like they all wore. Never mind about Yo-less saying it was all run by men in suits these days. One day, the world would hear from Wobbler Johnson – probably via a phone-line it didn't know was connected to its computer.

In the meantime, he was staring at columns of numbers in an effort to make a completely illegal copy of *Mr Bunky Goes Boing*. It had been given four stars and declared 'megabad!!!', which was what *Splaaaaatttt!* magazine still thought meant pretty good if you were under sixteen.

He blinked at the screen, and smeared the grease on his glasses a bit more evenly.

And that was enough for tonight.

He sat back, and his eye caught sight of *Only You Can Save Mankind*, under a pile of other discs.

Poor old Rubber. Of course, you called people mental all the time, but there *was* something weird about him. His body walked around down on Earth but his brain was probably somewhere you couldn't find with an atlas.

Wobbler shoved the disc in the drive. Odd about the game, though. There was probably a logical reason for it. That's what computers were, logical. Start believing anything else and you were in trouble.

The title came up, and then the bit that Gobi Software had pinched from *Star Wars*, and then—

His jaw dropped.

Ships. Hundreds of them. Getting bigger and bigger. Yellow ships, filling the screen, so that it was just black and yellow and just yellow and then blinding white—

Wobbler ducked.

And then a black screen.

Almost black, anyway.

For a moment the words hung there—

Hi, Wobler—

—and then vanished.

More alarms were clanging and whooping.

Kirsty peered out from between her fingers.

'I don't think we hit anyone,' said Johnny, tapping on the keys.

'You flew straight through them!'

'That's right!'

'OK, but they'll still come after us.'

'So *now* we turn round. It'll take a little while. How's the Captain?'

A clawed hand gripped the back of his chair, and her snout rested on his shoulder.

'This is very bad,' said the Captain. 'Our engines are not designed to run at this sort of speed for any length of time. They could break down at any moment.'

'It's a calculated risk,' said Johnny.

'Really? How precisely did you calculate it?' said the ScreeWee.

'Well . . . not exactly *calculate* . . . I just thought it was worth a try,' said Johnny.

'You're turning back towards the players!'

'And we're still accelerating,' said Johnny.

'What were you typing just then?' said Kirsty.

'Oh, nothing,' said Johnny, grinning. 'Just thought I saw someone I recognized. You know, as we flashed past.'

'Why are you looking so happy?' she demanded. 'We're in terrible trouble.'

'Dunno. Because it's *my* trouble, I suppose. Captain, why have all those lights over there come on?'

'They're the ships of the fleet,' said the Captain. 'The commanders want to know what's happening.'

'Tell them to hold on to something,' said Johnny. 'And tell them – tell them they're going home.'

They both looked at him.

'Oh, yes, *very* impressive,' said Kirsty. '*Very* dramatic. All very—'

'Shut up.'

'What?'

'Shut up,' said Johnny again, his eyes not leaving the screen.

'No-one tells me to shut up!'

'I'm telling you now. Just because you've got a mind like a, a *hammer* doesn't mean you have to treat everyone else like a nail. Now – here they come again . . .'

Wobbler took the disc out of the drive and looked at it. Then he felt around the back of his computer in case there were any extra wires.

That Johnny . . . he was the quiet type. He always said that all he knew about computers was how to switch them on, but *everyone* knew about computers. He'd probably messed around with the game and given it back. Pretty good. Wobbler wondered how he'd done it.

He put the disc back in and started the game again.

'Only You Can Save Mankind' . . . yeah, yeah.

Then the inside of the starship. Missiles, guns, score total, yeah, yeah . . .

And stars ahead. The sparkly ones you got in the game. He'd done much better ones for *Voyage to Alpha Centauri*.

No ships to be seen.

He picked up the joystick and moved it, watching the stars spin as the ship turned . . .

There was a ship right behind him. Very much behind him. Dozens of ships, again. *Hundreds* of ships. All getting bigger. Much bigger. Very quickly.

Very, very quickly.

Again.

When he got up off the floor and put the leg back on the chair, the screen was all black again, except for the little flashing cursor.

Wobbler stared at it.

Logic, he said. Not believing in logical reasons was

almost as bad as dropping hot solder on to a nylon sock. There had to be a logical explanation.

One day, he'd think of one.

'They're following us! They're following us!'

Little coils of smoke were coming up from the controls. There were all sorts of vibrations in the floor.

'I'm pretty sure we can outrun them,' said Johnny.

'How sure?' said Kirsty.

'Pretty sure.'

Kirsty turned to the Captain.

'Have we got any rear guns?'

The Captain nodded.

'They can be fired from here,' she said. 'But we should not do that. We have surrendered, remember?'

'*I* haven't,' said Kirsty. 'Which one fires the guns?'

'The stick with the button on the top.'

'This? It's just like a games joystick,' she said.

'Of *course* it is,' said Johnny. 'This is in our *heads*, remember. It has to be things we *know*.'

The screen showed the view behind the fleet. There were green ships bunched up behind them.

'They're coming right down our tailpipe,' said Kirsty. 'This is going to be really easy.'

'Yes, it is – isn't it,' said Johnny.

There was a dull edge to his voice. She hesitated.

'What do you mean?' she said.

'Just dots in the middle of a circle,' said Johnny. 'It's easy. Bang. Here comes the high score. Bang. Go ahead.'

'But it's game space! It's a *game*. Why are you acting like that? It's just something on a screen.'

'Fine. Just like the Real Thing. Press the button, then.'

She gripped the stick. Then she paused again.

'Why do you have to spoil everything?'

'Me?' said Johnny vaguely. 'Look, if you're not going to fire, switch the screen back to what's ahead of us, will you? This dial here says we're moving at $\vDash$ $\ominus$ per φ $\lesssim$, and that's $\not\subset$ times faster than it says we ought to be going.'

'Well?'

'Well, I just think it'd be nice not to run into an asteroid or something. Of course, if you want us to end up five miles across and one centimetre thick, keep looking back.'

'Oh, all *right*!'

She took her finger off the screen switch.

And then she gasped.

They stared at the expanse of space ahead of them, and what was in the middle of it.

'What,' said Kirsty, after a long pause, 'is *that*?'

Johnny laughed.

He tried to stop himself, because the ship was groaning and creaking like a tortured thing, but he couldn't. Tears ran down his cheeks. He thumped his hand helplessly on the control panel, accidentally switching a few lights on and off.

'It's the Border,' said the Captain.

'Yes,' said Johnny. 'Of course it is.'

'But it's—' Kirsty began.

'Yes,' said Johnny. 'The Border, see? Beyond it they're safe. Of course. *No-one* crosses the Border. Humans can't do it!'

'It can't be natural.'

'Who knows? This is game space, after all. It's probably natural here. I mean, we've all seen it before.'

'But it is still a very long way off,' said the Captain. 'I fear that—'

There was a dull explosion somewhere behind them.

'Missiles!' said Kirsty. 'You should have let me—'

'No, listen,' said Johnny. '*Listen.*'

'What to? I can't hear anything.'

'That's because something's making a lot of silence,' said Johnny. 'The engines have stopped.'

'The engines have probably melted,' said the Captain.

'We've still got . . . what is it . . . momentum or inertia or one of those things,' said Johnny. 'We'll keep going until we hit something.'

'Or something hits us,' said Kirsty.

She looked at the Border again.

'How big is that thing?' she said.

'It must be huge,' said Johnny.

'But there's stars beyond it.'

'Not our stars. I told you, that's one place humans can't go . . .'

They looked at one another.

'What happens, then,' Kirsty began, like someone exploring a particularly nasty hole in a tooth, 'if we're on a ship that tries to go past the Border?'

They both turned to the Captain, who shrugged.

'Don't ask me,' she said. 'It's never happened. It is impossible.'

Now all three of them turned to look at the Border again.

'Is it just me?' said Kirsty, 'or is it just a little bit bigger?'

There was some silence.

'Still,' said Johnny, 'what's the worst that can happen to us?'

Then he wished he hadn't said that. He remembered thinking he'd hear the alarm clock waking him up, that very first time, and then he recalled the shock of realizing that he wasn't being allowed to wake up at all.

'You know, I don't want to find out,' he added.

'Without engines, we cannot turn the ship around,' said the Captain. 'I am sorry. You were too keen to save us.'

'It *is* getting bigger,' said Kirsty. 'You can tell, if you watch the stars behind it.'

'I am sorry,' said the Captain again.

'At least the ScreeWee should make it,' said Johnny.

'I am sorry.'

Kirsty stood up. 'Well, *I'm* not,' she said. 'Come on!' She picked up the gun and strode away into the shadows. Johnny ran after her.

'Where do you think you're going?'

'To the escape capsule,' she said.

'What escape capsule?'

'Indeed,' said the Captain, scuttling after them, 'I ask that too. There is no such thing.'

'There can be if we want there to be,' said Kirsty, opening the door. 'You said the game is made up of things we know? Well, I *know* it'll be right down under the ship.'

'But—'

'It's my dream as well as yours, right? Believe me. There'll be an escape capsule.' Her eyes had that gleam again. She hefted the gun. 'I *know* it,' she said. 'I've been there.'

He remembered her room. He could picture her sitting there, with a dozen sharp pencils and no friends, getting top marks in her History homework, while in her head she was chasing aliens.

'I cannot understand,' said the Captain.

The corridor outside was full of steam. The ship might cross the Border, but it was going to have to have a lot of repairs before it ever came back.

'Um,' said Johnny. 'It's a bit like the models in the cereal packets. It's . . . kind of a human idea.'

The ScreeWee hesitated in the doorway. Then she turned to look at the screen.

'We are getting closer,' she said. 'If you think there is something there, then you must go now.'

'Come *on*!' said Kirsty.

'Uh—' Johnny began.

'Thank you,' said the Captain, gravely.

'I haven't really done much,' said Johnny.

'Who knows? You never thought of yourself. You tried to work things out. You made choices. And I chose well.'

'And now we must go!' said Kirsty.

'Perhaps we shall meet again. Afterwards. If all goes well,' said the Captain. She took one of Johnny's hands in two of her own.

'Goodbye,' she said.

Kirsty caught Johnny's shoulder and dragged him away.

'Nice to have met you,' she said to the alien. 'Sort of – interesting. Come on, you.'

Some of the lights had gone out. The corridors were full of steam and vague shapes. Kirsty ran on ahead, darting from shadow to shadow.

'We'll have to go down,' she said over her shoulder. 'It'll be there. Don't worry!'

'You're really into this, aren't you,' said Johnny.

'Here's a ramp. Come on. We can't have much time.'

There was another passage below that, and another

ramp, curling away down through the steam.

They came out in a room bigger than the bridge. There was a very large double door at one end, and banks of equipment around the walls. And, in the middle, standing on three landing legs, was a small ship. It had a stubby, heavy look.

'There! See? What did I tell you?' said Kirsty triumphantly.

Johnny walked over to the nearest equipment panel and touched it. It was sticky. He looked at his fingertips.

'It hasn't been here long,' he said. 'The paint's not dry.'

A screen in the middle of the panel lit up, showing the Captain's face.

'How interesting,' she said. 'I look down at my controls and discover a new one. You have found your escape capsule?'

'It looks like it,' said Johnny.

'We have ten minutes until we reach the Border,' said the Captain. 'You should have plenty of time.'

There was a whirring noise behind Johnny. The escape capsule's ramp was coming down.

'I found a switch on the landing leg,' said Kirsty.

He joined her. The ramp was a silvery grey-colour. It gleamed in the misty blue light that streamed down from inside the capsule.

'Can you guess what I'm thinking?' said Kirsty.

'You're thinking: We haven't seen the Gunnery Officer lately,' said Johnny. 'You're thinking: He'll be in there somewhere, hiding. Because this part is *your* dream, and that's how your dream works.'

'Only I'll be ready for him,' said Sigourney. 'Come on.'

She sidled up the ramp, turning constantly in a series of small excited hops to keep the gun pointed at any teeth that might suddenly appear.

There were two seats in the capsule, in front of a very small control panel. There was a big window. There were a couple of small cupboards. And there wasn't much of anything else.

Kirsty pointed to a cupboard and made a gesture to Johnny to open it. She raised her gun.

He opened the door and stood back quickly.

Kirsty seriously menaced a stack of tins.

She caught Johnny's expression.

'Well, he *could* have been in there,' she said.

'Oh, yes. Sure. Admittedly he'd have to stop to cut his arms and legs off and then curl up really small, but he could have been in there.'

'Hah! Smart comment!'

'Why not try looking under the seat cushions? It's amazing what goes down behind them.'

Kirsty tried to prod behind the control panel without Johnny noticing. He noticed.

'Maybe aliens don't watch the same kind of films we watch?' he said.

'All right, all right, no need to go on about it,' she snarled. She looked at the controls, and pressed a switch. The hatch swung up. The Captain's face appeared on a small screen in the middle of the panel.

'Eight minutes to the Border,' she said.

'Right,' said Kirsty. She shoved a hand down behind her seat cushion, and then looked at Johnny's grin.

'You see aliens everywhere, don't you,' he said.

'What's that supposed to mean?'

'Nothing. Nothing. Just a thought.'

She glowered at him.

There were seat belts. They put them on. Kirsty started to drum her fingers on the panel. She seemed to be looking for something.

'How do we open the doors?' said Johnny.

'All right, all right – it's got to be here somewhere.'

She pressed a button. Behind them, the ramp rose up and hissed into place.

Johnny looked around. There really *was* nowhere for anyone to hide. They were aboard the escape craft. They were safe.

He didn't *feel* safe. He grabbed Kirsty's arm.

'Wait a minute,' he said urgently. 'I think something's wro—'

The screen flickered into life.

There was a ScreeWee there.

It was the Gunnery Officer.

'Run and hide, human scum,' he said.

They could see the screen behind him; he was on the bridge.

'You? Where is the Captain?' said Johnny.

'She will be dealt with. While you run away.'

'No!'

Kirsty nudged him.

'Look, the ScreeWee are *safe*,' she said. 'The Border is only a few minutes away. We've done it all! You can't chase around after her now! She'll have to take her chances! That's what she'd say if you asked her!'

'But I can't ask her, can I?'

He reached over and pushed a switch. There was a whirring behind them as the ramp slid down.

'I'm going back up there,' he said.

'He'll be waiting for you!'

'Fine.' He picked up the alien gun. 'Which bit's the trigger?'

She rolled her eyes. 'This is stupid!'

'Scared, are you?' said Johnny. His face was pale.

'*Me?*' She shrugged and snatched the gun. 'I'll take this,' she said. 'I'm used to guns. You'll only make a mess of it.'

12

Just Like The Real Thing

They ran down the ramp and back to the corridor.

'Got a watch on?' said Johnny.

'Yes. We've got more than six minutes.'

'I should have *known*!' said Johnny, as they ran. '*No-one* gets that long to escape! James Bond never turns up with enough time to have a cup of coffee and clean his shoes before he disarms the time bomb! We're playing games again!'

'Calm down!'

'If we find a cat I'm going to kick it!'

The corridors were darker. Water dripped from the ceiling. There was still some steam, hissing out of broken pipes.

They reached a junction.

'Which way?'

Kirsty pointed.

'That way.'

'Are you sure?'

'Of course.'

They disappeared into the gloom.

About thirty seconds later they reappeared, running.

'Oh, yes, *of course*.'

'Well, they all look the same, *actually*. It must be this way!'

This one *did* lead to the wide corridor with the door to the bridge at the far end.

It was open. They could see the blue and white flickering of the big screen.

Kirsty changed her grip on the gun.

'O-*kay*,' she said. 'No messing about this time, right? No talking?'

'All right.'

'Let's go.'

'How?'

'You walk in there. When he leaps out at you, I'll get him.'

'Oh? I'm bait, am I?'

Kirsty glanced at her wrist.

'You've got four and half minutes to think of something better,' she said. 'Oh, sorry. Four minutes and twenty-five seconds. Hang on, that's twenty seconds now . . .'

'I just hope you're good!'

Kirsty patted the gun. 'Regional Champion, remember? Trust me.'

Johnny walked towards the open doorway. He tried to swivel his eyes both ways as he reached it.

'Four minutes and fifteen seconds,' said her voice, far, far behind him.

He halted on the threshold.

'How come you weren't National Champion?' he said.

'I had food poisoning on the day, *actually*.'

'Oh. Right.'

He stepped through.

Multi-toothed death failed to happen to him. He risked a better look to either side and then, swallowing, upwards as well.

'Nothing here,' he said.

'OK. I'm right behind you.'

On the screen the Border was already much bigger. We're travelling very fast, he thought, and it's still more than four minutes away, and already it's filling the sky. *Huge* isn't the word for it.

'I can see all round the room,' he said. 'No-one's here.'

'There was a control panel, wasn't there?' said Kirsty. 'Hang on . . . I'm in the doorway now. Yes. It's got to be behind the controls. Go ahead. I'm ready if it leaps out.'

I'm not, he thought. He sidled across the floor until he could just see behind the bank of instruments.

'There's noth . . . hold it.'

'What?'

'I think it's the Captain.'

'Is it alive?'

'She. She's a she. You know she's a she. I can't tell. She's just . . . lying there. I'll have a look.'

'What good would that do?'

'I'm going to have a look, all right?'

'Careful, then. Stay where I can keep an eye on you.'

He moved forward, searching the shadows around the edge of the huge room.

It was the Captain, and she was alive. At least, bits of what was probably her chest were going up and down. He knelt beside her.

'Captain?' he whispered.

She opened one eye.

'Chosen One?'

'What happened?'

'He was . . . waiting. While I . . . talked to you . . . he crept in . . . hit me . . .'

'Where'd he go then?'

'You . . . *must* . . . go. Not much time . . . left. The fleet . . . is . . .'

'You're hurt. I'll get Ki – Sigourney over here . . .'

Her claw gripped his arm.

'Listen to me! He's going . . . to blow up the . . . ship! The fuel . . . the power plant . . . he's . . .'

Johnny stood up.

'Is she all right?' Kirsty called out.

'I don't know!'

She was standing in the doorway, outlined against the light.

There was a shadow behind her. As Johnny watched, it spread its arms.

It was bigger than a ScreeWee should be, now. It wasn't a funny alligator – there was still a suggestion of alligator there, but now there was insect, too, and other things . . . things that had never existed outside of dreams . . .

Johnny shouted: 'He's behind you!' Then he lowered his head and ran.

Kirsty turned.

You can't *trust* dreams. If you live inside them, they'll turn on you, carry you along . . .

He saw Kirsty turn and look up, and up, at the Gunnery Officer.

The ScreeWee opened his mouth. There were more teeth than he'd had before; rows and rows of them, and every one glistening and sharp.

Her dream, Johnny thought. No wonder she always fights.

'Shoot it! Shoot it!'

She was just staring. She didn't seem to want to move.

165

'You've got the *gun*!' he screamed.

She was like a statue.

'*Shoot* it!'

'. . . oh . . .'

Kirsty shook her head vaguely and then, as if she'd suddenly clicked awake, raised the gun.

'OK,' she said. 'Now—'

The ScreeWee ignored her. He jerked his head up and focused on Johnny. He hardly had eyes, now. The alien seemed to be looking at Johnny with its teeth.

'Ah. The Chosen One,' it said. It slapped Kirsty out of the way. She couldn't even have seen its arm move. One moment she was aiming, and the next she was lifted into the air and dropping in a heap a few metres away.

The gun clattered on to the floor and slid towards Johnny.

'Chosen One!' hissed the ScreeWee. 'Foolish! We are what we are! You disgrace your race and mine! For you, and her . . . for you, there's no going back . . .'

Kirsty was trying to get to her feet, her face contorted with anger.

Johnny reached down and picked up the gun.

The ScreeWee waved two arms in a sudden movement. Johnny flinched.

He heard, from a long way away, Kirsty call out: 'Quick! Throw it to me! To *me*!'

The alien smiled.

Johnny backed away a little. The alien was concentrating entirely on him.

'To *me*, you idiot!' shouted Kirsty.

'You?' said the alien to Johnny. 'Shoot me? You can't. Such weakness. Like your Captain. A disgrace to the ScreeWee. Always weak. And that is why you want peace. The strong never want peace.'

Johnny raised the gun.

The alien moved forward, slowly. His teeth seemed to fill the world. His arms seemed longer, his claws sharper.

'You cannot,' it said. 'I've watched you. At least the other humans could fight! We could die honourably! But *you* . . . you *talk* and *talk* . . . you'd do anything rather than *fight*. You'd do anything but face the truth. *You* save mankind? Hah!'

Johnny stepped back again, and felt the edge of the control desk behind him. There was no more retreating.

'Will you surrender?' he said.

'Never!'

Johnny saw a movement out of the corner of his eye. Kirsty was going to try to leap on the thing. But the alien wasn't like the guards, now. She wouldn't stand a—

He fired.

There was a small, sharp explosion.

The ScreeWee looked down in shock at the sudden blue stain spreading across his overall, and then back up to Johnny almost in bewilderment.

'You *shot* me . . . in cold blood . . .'

'No. My blood's never cold.'

The alien toppled forward. And now he was smaller again, more like a ScreeWee.

'And I had to,' said Johnny.

'You shot him,' said the voice behind him. He looked round. The Captain had pulled herself to her feet.

'Yes.'

'You had to. But I didn't think you could . . .'

Johnny looked down at the gun. His knuckles were

white. With some difficulty, he managed to persuade his fingers to let go.

'I didn't think I could, either.'

He walked over to Kirsty, who was staring at the thing on the floor.

'Wow,' she said, but quietly.

'Yes,' he said.

'You—'

'Yes, I shot him. I shot him. I wish I didn't have to, but I had to. He was alive and now he isn't.' There were more alarms sounding now, and red lights flashing on the control panel. On the screen, the Border completely filled the sky. 'Can we go? How much longer have we got left?'

She looked hazily at her watch.

'A minute and a half.'

He was amazed. He felt he was sitting inside his own head, watching himself. There wasn't any panic. The one who was watching didn't know what to do, but the one outside seemed to know everything. It was . . . like a dream.

'Can you run?' She nodded. 'Really *fast*? What am I saying? You've probably won medals. Come on.'

He pulled her after him, out of the bridge and along the dark corridors. Kirsty was hardly concentrating any more; the walls glistened less. There were even nuts and bolts again.

They reached the capsule. Johnny ran from leg to leg until he found the button that let down the ramp. It seemed to take ages to come down.

'How long?'

'We've got fifty seconds . . .'

Up the ramp, into the seats.

There weren't many controls. Johnny peered at them.

'What are you doing?' said Kirsty.

'Like you said before. Looking for one marked "Doors Open".'

The screen flickered into life.

'Johnny? The doors open from up here,' said the Captain.

Johnny glanced up at Kirsty.

'We didn't know that,' he said.

'Is the ramp back up?'

'Yes.'

'Doors opening.'

There was a *clonk* ahead of them, and a hiss as the air in the hall escaped through the widening crack. The twinkling, unreal stars of game space beckoned them.

Johnny's hand hovered over the biggest red button on the panel.

'Johnny?'

'Yes, Captain.'

'Thank you. You did not have to help us.'

'If not me, then who else?'

'Hah. Yes. And now . . . goodbye. We will not . . . meet again.'

'Goodbye.'

Johnny looked at Kirsty.

'How long?'

'Ten seconds!'

'Let's go.'

He hit the button.

There was a *boom* behind them. The walls flashed past. And suddenly they were surrounded by sky.

Johnny leaned back against the seat. His mind was blank, empty, except for something which kept on replaying itself like a piece of film.

Over and over again, his memory fired the gun. Over and over again, the alien collapsed. Action replay. Pinpoint precision. Just like the Real Thing.

Kirsty nudged him.

'Can we steer it?'

'Hmm? What?' He looked vaguely at the controls. 'Well, there's this joystick . . .'

'Turn us round, then. I want to watch them go through.'

'Yes. Me too.'

The capsule turned gently in the deep void of game space, right up against the Border.

The ScreeWee fleet hurtled past. As each ship reached the Border it flickered and faded.

'Do you think they've got a planet to go to, really?'

'I think they think so.'

'Do you think they'll ever be back?'

'Not now.'

'Um . . . look . . . when I looked up and I saw that *thing* . . . I mean, it was so *real*. And I thought, but it's alive, it's living, how can I—'

'Yes,' said Johnny.

'And then it was dead and . . . and I didn't feel like cheering . . .'

'Yes.'

'When it's real, it's not easy. Because people die and it's really over.'

'Yes. I know. Over and over. D'you know what?'

'What?'

'My friend Yo-less thinks dreams like this are a way of dealing with real life.'

'Yes?'

'I think it's the other way round.'

170

'Yo-less is the black one?'

'Yes. We call him Yo-less because he's not cool.'

'Anti-cool's quite cool too.'

'Is it? I didn't know that. Is it still cool to say "well wicked"?'

'*Johnny!* It was *never* cool to say "well wicked".'

'How about "vode"?'

'Vode's cool.'

'I just made it up.'

The capsule drifted onwards.

'No reason why it can't be cool, though.'

'Right.'

Game stars glittered.

'Johnny?'

'Yes?'

'How come you get on with people so well? How come people always talk to you?'

'Dunno. Because I listen, I suppose. And it helps to be stupid.'

'Johnny?'

'Still here.'

'What did you mean . . . you know, back there? When you said I see aliens everywhere?'

'Um. Can't remember.'

'You must have meant *something*.'

'I'm not even sure there *are* aliens. Only different kinds of us. But I know what the important thing is. The important thing is to be exactly sure about what you're doing. The important thing is to remember it's not a game. None of it. Even the games.'

The ship became a dot against the night.

'What do we do to get home? I've always had to die to get out.'

'You can get out if you win.'

171

'There's a green button here.'

'Worth a try, yes?'

'Right.'

Light was streaming into the room when Johnny woke up. He lay in someone else's bed and looked around through half-closed eyes.

It was like all spare rooms everywhere. There was the lamp that was a bit old-fashioned and didn't fit in anywhere else. There was the bookcase with the books that no-one read much. There was a lack of *small* things, apart from an ashtray on the bedside table.

There was a clock, but at some time in the past the mains had gone off for a while and although people must have sorted out every other clock in the house, they'd forgotten about this one, so it just sat and flashed 7:41 continuously, day and night. But an absence of sound from below suggested that it was still early in the morning.

He snuggled down, treasuring this time stolen between dreaming and waking.

So . . . what next? He'd have to talk to Kirsty, who dreamed of being Sigourney and forgot that she was trying to be someone who was *acting*. And he had a suspicion that he'd see his parents before long. He was probably going to be talked at a lot, but at least that'd make a change.

These were still Trying Times. There was still school. Nothing actually was better, probably. No-one was doing anything with a magic wand.

But the fleet had got away. Compared to that, everything else was . . . well, not easy. But less like a wall and more like steps.

You might never win, but at least you could try. If not you, who else?

He turned over and went back to sleep.

The Border hung in the sky.

Huge white letters, thousands of miles high. They spelled:

And the fleet roared past. Tankers, battleships, fighters . . . they soared and rolled, their shadows streaking across the letters as ship after ship escaped, for ever.

TITLES BY TERRY PRATCHETT
AVAILABLE FROM CORGI BOOKS

THE PRICES SHOWN BELOW WERE CORRECT AT THE TIME OF GOING TO PRESS. HOWEVER TRANSWORLD PUBLISHERS RESERVE THE RIGHT TO SHOW NEW RETAIL PRICES ON COVERS WHICH MAY DIFFER FROM THOSE PREVIOUSLY ADVERTISED IN THE TEXT OR ELSEWHERE.

☐	52595 2	**TRUCKERS**	£3.99
☐	52586 3	**DIGGERS**	£2.99
☐	52649 5	**WINGS**	£2.99
☐	52752 1	**THE CARPET PEOPLE**	£3.99
☐	12475 3	**THE COLOUR OF MAGIC**	£3.99
☐	13945 9	**THE COLOUR OF MAGIC** (Graphic Novel)	£7.99
☐	12848 1	**THE LIGHT FANTASTIC**	£3.99
☐	13105 9	**EQUAL RITES**	£3.99
☐	13106 7	**MORT**	£4.99
☐	13107 5	**SOURCERY**	£3.99
☐	13460 0	**WYRD SISTERS**	£4.99
☐	13461 9	**PYRAMIDS**	£3.99
☐	13462 7	**GUARDS! GUARDS!**	£4.99
☐	13463 5	**MOVING PICTURES**	£4.99
☐	13464 3	**REAPER MAN**	£4.99
☐	13465 1	**WITCHES ABROAD**	£3.99
☐	13890 8	**SMALL GODS**	£4.99
☐	13703 0	**GOOD OMENS** (co-written with Neil Gaiman)	£4.99
☐	13325 6	**STRATA**	£3.99
☐	13326 4	**THE DARK SIDE OF THE SUN**	£3.99

All Corgi Books are available at your bookshop or newsagent, or can be ordered from the following address:

Transworld Publishers Ltd,
Cash Sales Department,
P.O. Box 11, Falmouth, Cornwall TR10 9EN

Please send a cheque or postal order (no currency) and allow £1.00 for postage and packing for one book, an additional 50p for a second book, and an additional 30p for each subsequent book ordered to a maximum charge of £3.00 if ordering seven or more books.

Overseas customers, including Eire, please allow £2.00 for postage and packing for the first book, an additional £1.00 for a second book, and an additional 50p for each subsequent title ordered.

NAME: ....

ADDRESS: ....

....

TRUCKERS

Terry Pratchett

To the thousands of tiny nomes who live under the floorboards of a large department store, there is no Outside. Things like Day and Night, Sun and Rain are just daft old legends.

Then a devastating piece of news shatters their existence: the Store – their whole world – is to be demolished. And it's up to Masklin, one of the last nomes to come into the Store, to mastermind an unbelievable escape plan that will take all the nomes into the dangers of the great Outside . . .

The first title in a marvellously inventive fantasy trilogy.

Shortlisted for the *Smarties* Prize.

0 552 52595 2